The Animals of Paradise

Noura Durkee

بسم الله
Ha... bless you all ways
Noura Durkee

illustrated by Simon Trethewey

HOOD HOOD BOOKS

Copyright © Hood Hood Books 1996

Hood Hood Books
29 Bolingbroke Grove
London SW11 6EJ

British Library Cataloguing-in-Publication Data.
A catalogue for this book is available from the British Library.

ISBN 1 900251 09 4 (PB)
ISBN 1 900251 25 6 (HB)

Designed and Pageset by Linda Males
Origination Medialine S.A.L./ClockWise
Printed in Hong Kong

Contents

Adam
Noah
Salih
Abraham
Ishmael
Moses
David
Solomon
Jonah
Jesus
Muhammad

Dear Earthly Friends:

I am writing to you this short note to introduce the stories of The Animals of Paradise, which I recorded in those lovely early days when they first arrived here and were getting to know one another. History is different in Paradise, you know – you can go backwards or forwards or sideways in time, and live wherever you please.

I'm just a junior recording angel. My task is to record the sayings and doings of all the animals, especially those connected to all our prophets from Adam to Muhammad, may peace be on them all. You will see that the prophets are very important in these tales. Solomon and Moses have particularly strong relationships with the animals, and you will find their names mentioned often. I listened to these stories just as they were buzzed or chirped or baaa-ed or barked during those early days of the meetings in the Garden. That keeps me pretty busy, chasing them all over the place, but it is quite a pleasure as well. There are a lot of animals here, for all animals enter Paradise. I'm happy to be with the animals while I gain experience. Only senior angels have the complicated job of guarding people!

You might like to know where you can find these stories outside of Paradise. The beasts and birds and insects and fish who told these stories were remembering experiences from their lives on earth. Most of the tales were so important that they have been told in the Quran. Elephant has a whole chapter named after him, and so do some of the others. But the Quran leaves out a lot of details which are filled in from different traditions. I did put in some descriptions from my own experiences on earth while I was looking after the animals. And of course, the animals themselves remembered many small details an angel might have missed.

Angelic Introduction

Some animals, like Sheep and Cow, had so many stories, they had to choose which ones to tell. Others, like Horse, though his name is mentioned in many places, has really no tale of his own, so he tells a story from Arab tradition.

Welcome to Paradise, my earthly friends! I hope you enjoy the tales, and may God and all the animals please forgive me for any mistakes I've made in the telling.

With love to you all,
The Recording Angel

All Together in Paradise

"I'm so happy to be here!" announced Wolf as he stretched out on the cool green grass. "I had a really hard life on earth. People were always thinking I was the bad guy – can you imagine? They even accused me of eating the Prophet Joseph when he was a little boy! Who did they think I was, anyway? As if I'd harm a hair of his holy head ..."

Donkey was kicking her feet lazily in the air after a good roll. "That's nothing," she said. "I had to carry their boxes and bags and bundles. I was quite patient, but, when it got to be too much, I complained. Then they used to cover their ears and criticise me for having an ugly voice! I have a beautiful voice. Would you like to hear it?"

"No, thank you," said Wolf hastily. "This is Paradise, remember? You have nothing to complain about here. Look, here comes my cousin, Dog. Peace be with you, Cousin!"

"Peace, peace,peace!" panted Dog. "I've been running and running over these green hills, and drinking from sweet springs, and sniffing all these lovely new smells. I think I'll flop down here and take a nap with you two."

"That's a habit of yours, Cousin," laughed Wolf. "I seem to remember a nap you took that went on for three hundred years or so...more or less."

"Ah, that was a nap, that was," yawned Dog. "Perhaps we can talk about it later...?" He turned around a few times in a bed of moss and fell asleep immediately.

Wolf looked at Donkey. "He's always like that, you know. Sleeps whenever he can. Good old fellow!"

"Yes, I've always worked well with Dog," said Donkey. "I'd like to know the story of that long nap, though. Do you think we might wake him up?"

"No, no!" laughed Wolf. "I have to remind you again, this is Paradise. He can do whatever he likes. Anyhow, here come some more friends, Lion and Cow! Sit down! Isn't it interesting talking together like this? On earth we'd be eating each other up...Who's that hiding behind the rose-bushes?"

"It's Sheep, poor thing," said Cow quietly. "She's afraid of Wolf and Lion, and a lot of the others as well. She just can't get used to being safe at last. I tried to tell her that you were all harmless now, but she kept looking at your teeth, you know."

"This will never do," said Wolf anxiously. "We can't go on being afraid of one another – of course, I'm never afraid of anybody, but I can imagine – we must do something. Shall I play dead?" And he rolled over on his back and put his feet in the air.

"You don't look very dead," said Donkey. "I know, because I died once and they used my bones to prove a miracle."

"I didn't realise you had a story too," said Wolf. "We really must think of a way to share our experiences. But now, about this scared sheep, what if I just go and drag her out of the bush...?"

"Heavens, no! You'll frighten her even more!" mooed Cow. "Just wait a moment, I'll see what I can do. I really had to make sure of your intentions first, you know." Cow ambled over to the bush and the others could hear muffled mooings and baaings and bleating until, at last, the white woolly form of Sheep could be seen emerging from behind the roses. She walked timidly over to the group, being careful to keep the large comforting body of Cow between herself and the wolf.

"I am sorry I didn't trust you," bleated Sheep. "but after a lifetime of fear, it's difficult to change one's views."

"Never mind," said Wolf. "We understand. It's just that we're having this little get-together and don't want anyone to feel left out. We all feel a little strange. I mean, it's hard for me not to imagine making a short leap over Cow and..."

"Oh, oh, help!" cried Sheep, taking off in the direction of the rose-bush.

"See here," said Lion severely, speaking for the first time. "You really must not

do that, friend Wolf. We of the teeth and claws can't expect the others to understand our rather raw humour. Anyway, you're not hungry, are you?"

"No, I'm not, and that's really peculiar," mused Wolf. "I mean, as long as I can remember, I've always been hungry. But still, just the idea of a fat sheep dinner..."

"Stop it, I say!" growled Lion. "Now we're not going to have any fuss. I know you wouldn't do anything to Sheep, but you must be more sensitive to the others' feelings. COME ON BACK, SHEEP! No one's going to hurt you! What a timid creature you are!"

"I can't help it," whispered Sheep, sidling back to her seat beside Cow. "We are who we are. God gave me a certain nature and if I can't be natural here, where can I be?"

"There, there," said Cow. "It's all right now. Look, here comes the hoopoe!"

Hoopoe sailed down to a low branch and caught his breath before greeting them all with the greetings of Paradise. He seemed a little ruffled and his feathers needed preening. "I'm sorry to be so unpresentable," he said. "It's because of the air here. It is really amazing to fly in it. It's almost as if you could eat it, or, or – drink it. And it holds you up with no effort at all. I got so, well, drunk on it that I was doing flip-flops and somersaults and high dives! Excuse me," and he proceeded to straighten his plumage.

Lion chuckled. "I've noticed that myself," he said in his low, majestic voice. "I've been chasing my tail like a cub, for no reason at all, and I saw Dog running after butterflies a little while ago. Where is Dog, anyway?"

"He's over there asleep in the moss," said Wolf lazily. "He said he'd tell us his story later...and that brings up a subject I'm interested in. I didn't know some of you on earth, at least not very well. I suppose for obvious reasons. Because of my habits, I mean. My eating habits, that is. It's all right, Sheep. But now that we're here, and all past rivalries and, ah, tastes, are to be forgotten (here Wolf looked a little sad), perhaps we could get better acquainted. You know, nothing formal. But a shared story or two, a walk together in the woods (here Sheep looked decidedly uneasy), a romp on the grass...something to bring us closer

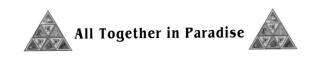

together. I'd like that. I've been rather lonely, to be truthful. I don't know how you others feel about it..."

"Why Wolf, I think you're blushing!" said Cow. "We never knew you were lonely. How could we? You were always so...but enough of that!"

"Ahem," said Lion. "If it's quite all right with you all, and I'm not stepping on anybody's toes, I'd like to make a suggestion." And he looked politely at his large paws, claws sheathed.

"Of course," said Hoopoe. "We are all, I think, listening."

"Well then, how about a story hour?" purred Lion. "We haven't any schedules here, after all. We don't have any other appointments or obligations. Why don't we meet every day here on this lovely grass, and take turns telling our stories from earth? It would be very interesting and would give us a chance to get to know one another. Eternity is a long time, at least I think so, and we needn't hurry."

"Oh goody!" brayed Donkey. "Now, can I wake up Dog?"

"Let's wait until tomorrow," purred Lion softly. "That will give us all time to prepare our stories. Just now I feel like another long run across those hills...goodbye!"

The others lay on the grass talking for a little while. Hoopoe agreed to tell the birds and other flying creatures, and Horse, who came up late happily frisking his tail, said he would run around and find the other animals. So they went their separate ways, in ones and twos, still amazed and bewildered by their blessings. Each one was also thinking very hard of the most important story he or she could tell from their life on earth.

When all the animals had gone, a little ant poked her head out of the grass. "Well," she said to herself, "I know I can't die twice, but I was quite worried for a while. Paradise or not, big feet are big when seen from an ant's eye. I'm glad they are gone to romp somewhere else! Now I'll have time to get a proper house ready before the meeting tomorrow. Indeed, I too have a story to tell!" And she disappeared into the nearby flower bed.

Dog and the Long Sleep

I think you should know why Lion was chosen as Leader. Everyone knows how kingly Lion is. He is just a natural-born leader. And since he had no story of his own to relate, he could listen to the others without having to prepare one himself. The meeting did need an arbiter to get everyone organised and quiet at the same time, and to start and stop the stories, and so forth. Lion's regal appearance and his marvellous roar made him perfect for this role.

Dog's story appears in the Quran as 'The People of the Cave', and it is found in earlier traditions as well. It is about people with faith in God being persecuted and chased out of their homes by others who do not want to change. By a miracle they are saved and find other people who are more sympathetic to their belief.

Recording Angel

The next day, the animals assembled eagerly to hear and tell their stories. The very first to arrive was the spider, who had gone unnoticed the day before as she hung from a bit of silk in the tree. She decided to build a suitable web from which to speak, and was hard at work on her design when Cow and Sheep arrived, bringing Camel. Camel, being tall, nearly ran into the web but stopped in time. "I'm sorry," he said, "I didn't mean to frighten you."

"That's all right," said Spider. Oddly, her voice was loud enough for Camel to hear, although a bit squeaky. "They're disposable, you know. But I find that here the designs that come into my head are quite extraordinary. I really am outdoing myself. Look, see the details of the pattern in the corner, there by your left ear?" Camel looked. Indeed, the web was remarkable. It was very fine and

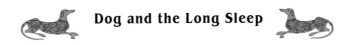

very large. Instead of the usual geometry, it had arabesques of floral patterns around the edges, and two or three layers of octagons in different thickness of silk. Camel was suitably impressed and walked around the web carefully after complimenting its maker.

Hoopoe flew up with Raven and Bee. Snake curled around a rock in the sun. Ant was there, sitting on top of a freshly built ant-hill which was very large and perfectly symmetrical.

The last to arrive was Donkey, and she was carrying something. She had baskets slung across her back with two big jars in them. "I never thought I would do this again willingly," she said, "but how else was Fish to come? So I filled these with some of that lovely water, and he's inside one of them. I don't remember which one. The other is just for balance, you know. There's nothing I dislike more than an unbalanced load." She stood patiently so as not to slosh the water.

The creatures formed themselves into a sort of circle, with the smaller ones in front and the birds and so forth in the trees, whose branches conveniently overhung the lawn. Out of long habit, Lion placed himself at the focal point of the group, on a slight rise of land where he could lie on a big rock, head on paws, in the warm sunshine.

The hoopoe, always the politician from his long years at court, noticed immediately that some sort of leader would be needed if this meeting was really to take place in an orderly fashion. He looked around the group and considered who could do it best. Someone who didn't talk too much. Someone who was a good listener. Someone who commanded authority. Clearly, Lion was the best choice. While all the others were fluffing their feathers, scratching, talking to their neighbours, and otherwise getting settled, he flew over to Lion and whispered something in his ear.

Hoopoe then stepped forward and flapped his wings. "Listen, everybody!" he called. "It's wonderful that we're all here together! If you could just listen a moment..." Some of the animals heard him, and some didn't. The general commotion went on: greetings between old friends, shy introductions, rustling

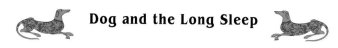

of papers (some of the animals had brought prepared speeches), and the like. Lion listened and then sat up rather abruptly. He yawned, such a tremendous, enormous, magnificent yawn, that everybody came to attention and all the noise stopped. While they were all looking in stunned amazement, Lion spoke.

"It has been suggested that I chair this meeting. I have not sought this honour, and there may be others more suitable to take it (here Lion looked around modestly), however, I would be willing..." Here Lion's voice trailed off and he waited. The other animals looked at one another for a moment and then suddenly Donkey brayed in pleasure. Cow mooed. Dog woke up and barked. The birds whistled, chirped and cheeped. Fish flapped his tail. All in all, there was a general statement of agreement to the idea. Hoopoe retired quietly to a branch over Lion's head, and Lion himself looked around the circle with obvious satisfaction.

"All right then," he said with a low rumble in the throat. "I see it's the will of the majority, so I will take on this responsibility. Who's going to be first?" There was silence as Lion looked around the circle. "Who wants to be first?" he purred. "Don't be bashful, now. We want to hear everyone's story, and somebody must begin!"

But somehow everybody felt shy. Even the most outspoken ones were a little in awe of Lion, and the setting, and the occasion. After all, this was the very first time they had all been together since the Ark. They all knew that in Paradise only the truth may be spoken, and they weren't even sure themselves what would come out of their mouths. So, although there was a good deal of shifting and shuffling, nobody offered to be first.

"Come, come," laughed Lion. "Who's to begin?"

Wolf spoke up: "Let Dog begin! He gave us the idea in the first place!"

They all looked around for Dog. "He's asleep again," sighed Donkey. "Good old fellow. There he is, in the flower bed." And Donkey got up and nudged Dog gently with her soft nose.

"Yes – no – hmmmph – what?" said Dog. "Good morning, everybody. What's up?"

"You're up, silly old thing," said Donkey, "and everybody is waiting to hear your story!"

"Oh, my story," said Dog. "It's not much, really. In fact, I was asleep most of the time. I'm sure somebody else will have a more interesting one."

"No, no," came the chorus from all sides. "You begin, Dog!" So Dog shook himself all over, yawned and strolled into the centre of the circle where he sat down on his haunches. He looked around with a serious expression. All the animals were waiting. There was, for once, complete silence. "Ahem," said Dog, clearing his throat. There were a few cheers of encouragement from the audience. "Well," said Dog softly. There were a few shouts of "Louder!" and "We can't hear!" and finally Dog began...

"I wasn't very old, scarcely more than a puppy, when my dear master bought me and took me to his house. I loved him from the first minute. I loved his strong hands and his gentle voice. I loved to play with him, to get things for him, and to follow him everywhere. I loved him so much that I was always concerned about his safety. At first I only protected him from cats and butterflies, but as I grew older, and began to understand the duties of a good dog, I tried to protect him from every kind of danger. I was especially careful of strange people and newcomers. I wouldn't let anyone near his house until he told me they were friends.

"And my master did have friends. They came often and they spent a lot of time talking. Sometimes their talk was happy and filled with laughter, but at other times it was serious. As time went on, their talking became more and more serious. I couldn't hear all of it, because of course I was outside guarding the house and the door. However, I did pick up bits here and there. It seemed that in the world of people there were a lot of differences of opinion. My master and his friends were believers, of course. They were trying their best to live by God's laws. But a lot of other people were breaking those laws and didn't seem to care. This made my master and his friends very sad.

"But that wasn't all. Those other people didn't like my master and his friends.

I heard something about threats, punishments, and such like. I didn't catch exactly what. Sometimes one or another of them would come, and I could smell pain in him, and several times I saw that one was injured as if he had been hit by a stone or struck with a stick. I never could understand exactly what was happening.

"At last there came a time when my master and his companions decided that they couldn't live in that place any longer. They seemed to be very sad. I couldn't see why anyone would be sad to leave a place where the people hit you with stones and sticks and argued with you. However, I was only a dog and did not know why people do what they do. I only knew I loved my master. So they left, and I of course went too. They didn't take much with them.

"We walked for a long time. We were climbing up into the hills, heading towards a cave that they knew, a safe place where nobody else ever went. It was a secret place, far from the town and the roads of men, and only known by those who went alone into the hills. At last, when we were very tired, we reached that place.

"They decided to take a nap there in the cave, and to awaken in the evening when it was cooler. I think perhaps they were afraid of the people seeing them, as well. Anyway, they wouldn't let me bark or run around all the way up, and I had a sense of danger from them that kept me on my guard for trouble. But none came.

"They were all really quite worn out, and fell asleep quickly. I stayed awake for a while, looking about and sniffing. I wanted to be sure no one was coming up the path from below, because they seemed a bit worried about people following them from the town. Finally, I lay down right across the mouth of the cave, and stretched out my paws in the entrance, so as to be sure no one came to bother my master. After a while I, too, fell asleep. I must say that was a wonderful sleep. I've never had such a good rest, and the dreams...well.

"So, after however long it was, we all woke up more or less at once. I'm sure everyone had been asleep while I was, and no person or animal came to disturb us, or I would have known. I have, after all, a very keen sense of smell, and it doesn't sleep. All the young men felt very refreshed, but they couldn't tell quite how long they had been sleeping. One thought it was a day, or part of a day. Others said that only God knew. Anyhow, they were very hungry, but they didn't want to go on to the nearest village all together. They didn't want to be seen as a group. So they chose one of them to go down the other side of the mountain and look for some food. They gave him some silver money to buy bread. They all warned him to be very careful and not get noticed. They were afraid of the bad people, you see. They sent me with him as protection, and I was proud to go.

"So we went on and soon found a small town. There was a bakery there, and my man went in. He found some bread he wanted, but, when he tried to pay for it, the baker wouldn't take his money. He said it was too old! I thought he must be crazy. But he thought my man was crazy. He called in his wife, and his son, and his neighbours, and they were all carrying on about this money. They also seemed amazed by the clothes my man was wearing. They kept walking around him, and pointing at this and that. I must say they themselves looked a little strange to me, but I am no judge of people's fashions and we dogs, thank goodness, don't have to wear those things.

"My young man kept trying to tell them that he just wanted to buy some bread, and he was quite alarmed at all the fuss they were making. He couldn't get them to believe his story. They even thought his language was strange! Finally, they took him to the mayor of the town and the judge and they had him tell his story all over again for the fifth time. All these important people looked at the money, and the clothes, and listened carefully to his speech. Then all together they picked themselves up and went back up the mountain with us. They did remember to bring some bread, but I don't know what happened to the money.

"When we reached the cave, we found all the others hiding, scared that the townspeople were like those other ones with their sticks and stones. But, happily, these ones were different. They listened to the story again, and looked around the cave, and shook their heads, and then they explained why they were so surprised to see us. It seems that the money, and the clothes, and even my

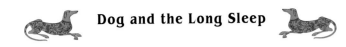

master's voice, were from another time. It seems they were very, very old. It seems that we had all been asleep in that cave for ... hundreds of years!

"Anyhow, the best part was that the bad people from the other town were all dead and gone and my master and his friends found themselves among believers. These people knew that we were part of a miracle! My men were honoured and respected by them. Even I was treated very well, never kicked or made to stay out in the rain. Only they seemed a little shy of touching us, as if we might break or something. But my master felt right at home among them, and soon learned to talk just as they did, and prayed with them and everything. So I guess he had found his people and didn't have to be afraid any more. He seemed much happier and I didn't hear any more worried discussions in the night. I didn't smell the fear any longer. My master was happy, so I was happy. And that's the end of my tail wagging to say that's the end of my tale. Now if you don't mind, I'm going back to sleep."

Dog bowed slightly and went back to his bed in the flowers. As he passed by, the animals nodded their approval and pleasure at his tale. All this talk of sleep had made everyone feel a little nappish, so they were happy when Lion announced that they would adjourn for the day and meet again tomorrow for the next story.

The Donkey Who Died

Now Donkey is going to tell how she once died and was brought back to life. She will tell it just as she heard it from her master. I do not think people remember how very important Donkey has been. But Cow and Camel do. Cow watched Jesus' entry into Jerusalem on Palm Sunday on Donkey. Camel witnessed Halima, the Bedouin nurse, taking Muhammad on Donkey from Mecca out into the desert to be raised in her tribe, as was the custom of the Arabs at that time.

Recording Angel

The next day the animals gathered again in the same spot. They found all the grass and flowers renewed, and no signs of their sitting or eating. In fact, everything seemed to be more beautiful and more abundant than before. There were fresh berries on the bushes that got no fewer, no matter how many the birds ate. The flower bed in which Dog had slept was blooming with violets and pansies. Not a stem was broken. And all around Ant's house there was a tall growth of purple iris, to keep off the unwary foot or hoof. Best of all, there was a small pond set about with stones, white sand and water lilies, so that Fish could have a home and Donkey could rest.

Donkey was so grateful that she went frisking about, waving her tail, and when Lion sat down and the meeting started, she offered to tell the next story.

"Dog's tale reminded me of my own," she began shyly. "Both of us had the strange experience of sleeping for a long, long time. But there are some differences between us, which I will try to explain. I hope you understand that my story won't be quite so clear as Dog's. That's not only because he's a better public speaker, which he is (here several animals kindly shook their heads). It's

because I was really truly completely dead. So I don't remember all of what went on. If you know what I mean.

"That is, some of it I had to be told about later. But I pieced it together afterwards and, to the best of my knowledge, this is what happened to me.

"I too had a master. He was a nice enough man; he didn't overload me, and he gave me oats to eat sometimes and even a little hot mash when the weather was very cold. I considered myself lucky. If you knew the sad life of some of my kind – but that's another story. Anyway, my master and I were walking along one day on a deserted road and we passed by a small village. I was hoping to see some other donkeys, as there are usually lots of us in villages. But there were none in this place. There were no people, either, or dogs. The place was ruined. The roofs had fallen into the houses. The mud walls were melting into the earth. The streets and paths were filled with rubble and rubbish. The trees and plants had gone wild and then had died.

"Altogether it was a scene of desolation. There was no life to be seen in it.

"Now my master believed in God. But his belief was a little unclear. He believed more in what he could see and touch, and in what was in front of his nose, if you know what I mean. Like a donkey who has to eat the grass by the side of the road because she won't believe that dinner and a warm barn are around the next turn in the road. So my master looked at this ruined town and said, 'Oh! How could God bring all this to life after its death?'

"Now that's all I personally remember until towards the end of the story. But I heard all the rest from my master, who told it many, many times, and I have no reason to disbelieve him. When my master said, 'Oh! How could God bring all this to life after its death?' God put him to death. He was really quite dead. He remained dead for a hundred years! However, for him, it was a very, very deep sleep. Now, while he was dead, I also was dead. I remember falling over dead, and I remember thinking, 'So, now I'm dead,' and then I don't remember anything because there was nothing to remember. Everything stayed the same; I heard no sounds; there was nothing. And I had been carrying some food in one of my baskets. You know how fruit spoils after a day or two, especially if it

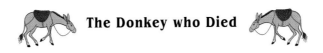

has fallen on the ground out of a basket! And how bread gets dried up and eaten by birds or turns into dust? Very strangely, this particular food didn't spoil at all. It just stayed there. So did my master's drink. It stayed in its bottles for a hundred years with no change.

"When my master woke up – for he thought he was just waking from a nap – God asked him, 'How long have you been here?' My master was puzzled. He answered, 'Perhaps a day or part of a day.'

"God told him, 'No, you have been here a hundred years! But look at your food and your drink; they show no signs of age. And look at your donkey.' I, having been dead a hundred years, was nothing but bones and a few bits of hair. God explained that He was going to make my master a sign for the people. In this, my master was like the people in Dog's cave.

"Then God told my master to look at the bones. As he was looking, God put them all back in their rightful places and covered them with flesh, and skin, and hair, and my mane and my tail and my ears (here Donkey waved her lovely soft ears gently back and forth). My Ears! And he brought me all back to life and breathed into me and I was there again as good as new. Now nobody can explain that. It's just God's business. And my master knew that and saw that and he said,

"I know now that God is able to do all things."

"So that was a good lesson for him. As for me, I was quite surprised and delighted to find myself in one piece. I wanted to move on to a less deserted place where the grass was greener. And we did. Everywhere we went, as I said, my master told the story over and over. He was so convincing – after all, it really did happen just as I've told you – that many people came to believe in the power of God because of it. And I'm glad of that. I mean, that I could be of some service. I do like to be of service. So thank you all very much for listening."

There was complete silence after Donkey's story. Nobody had known that gentle Donkey had been through such an amazing experience. Then everybody started talking at once, and touching Donkey's ears, and her nose, and thanking her. She became quite embarrassed and kept saying she had nothing to do with it. But Cow decided to add something.

The Donkey who Died

"Did you know," she mooed happily, "that our beloved Donkey had other honours? Not only did she take part in a miracle, she got to carry Jesus on her back!" The others fell silent again and listened. Cow continued:

"When Jesus came to the city of Jerusalem, the people were waiting expectantly to see him. They were in a joyous mood and felt such love in their hearts that they lined the pavement of the streets with flowers and palm branches. I know because I used to graze in the fields among the olive trees, and I saw them. Jesus approached the city from a hill known as the Mount of Olives, and he came down to the people riding on Donkey. She had a wreath of flowers around her neck. I followed after the crowd and ate some of the flowers, too."

"Not only that!" announced Camel. "Donkey also carried another Prophet! Some poor Bedouin came into Mecca with her, and I saw them from the desert where I lived. Donkey looked all skin and bones, hungry, dusty and tired out. I felt very sorry for her. The people with her did not look much better, either. I went on grazing on some thorn bushes, and then later that day I saw Donkey again. But I had to blink all two pairs of my eyelashes to be sure I was seeing the same beast. She was prancing along, sleek and fat, moving quickly and cheerfully. The woman on her back was changed also. She was carrying two babies, and all three of them were laughing, and so was the man who walked beside. I was amazed. Later I met Donkey and asked her what had happened that day, and she explained that the people went to town to find a baby to feed and nurse. As soon as they took this baby, everything changed for them and for Donkey too. They called the baby Muhammad."

The animals all nodded to each other. If someone got to carry prophets around, and if that same someone were chosen for a miracle, God must think highly of them. They were all impressed.

Then they went off happily for their various heavenly lunches, and Donkey went off with her friend Cow to find an even greener spot on which to graze.

Horse Explains Why

Dog and Donkey listened carefully and were able to tell what happened to them and their masters without leaving out much. They did a good job of reporting the human side of their tails, excuse me, tales. Horse did, too, although perhaps he did not know one thing. What Ishmael did to him was done quite on purpose, to find the most loyal and trustworthy animals. It probably hurt Ishmael as much as it hurt them, but he had to do it, so he could breed the bravest and most beautiful horse – the Arab horse.

Recording Angel

The next day Horse pranced up to the front of the group. He shook his mane, waved his magnificent tail, stamped his forefoot and whinnied. "I want to say," said Horse, "that some of us have had a very special relationship with humans. Dog (and he arched his lovely neck in Dog's direction) has told of his adventures as guardian and companion. My sweet cousin Donkey (here he smiled down at her) has served people patiently for centuries. Amazing as it may seem, some of us, and I include here my half-brother Mule, our dear Donkey and my esteemed friend Camel, have actually allowed men and women to ride upon our backs.

"God made us for beauty, but He also made us to ride. Even the angels ride angelic horses; the Archangel Gabriel, rides a horse named Hin Hiyawin, whom I am now very proud to name my friend.

"This riding action does not come about automatically. First, we have to let them catch us. That game is interesting for a while. Then, we let them put things on us: blankets, which I happen to like, saddles, which are not bad, and bridles, which are rather nasty. We let them do this because these pieces of equipment allow them to communicate better with us. Some can ride without them, but they are the exceptions. And after that, we let them get upon our broad strong backs and go for a ride.

"Why we do this, I have often wondered. Of course they repay us with oats and apples and warm houses in winter. But that is not our reason. Now the others may say what they will, and their turns will come, but I have my own ideas. I just simply love to have a rider on my back. It makes me feel complete somehow. It's like having an extra mind, one full of exciting ideas and directions. It's like being half horse and half human both at once. And a good rider, I'm sure, feels half human and half horse. I enable riders to go places they couldn't get to without me. Riders enable me to have all sorts of adventures and to think as a person, which I can't do without them. It's a wonderful relationship.

But it was wrong of so many of them to be so attached to me. They used to put their mark on my back and say I belonged to them. Foolish people. They are most forgetful. They love me almost as much as they love their wives and their children and their stored-up heaps of gold and silver. They love me the way people love who have almost forgotten everything else. But, I will say in their defence, horses are very loveable. And we love the humans as well.

"Did you know we were one of the tests God sent to Solomon? Once that Prophet had some of my brothers in his stables. One day, he had us paraded before him so that he could admire our beauty and grace. We delighted him so much that he suddenly realised he had forgotten God! He was thinking only of his own possessions. We were led away, but then he called for us to return, and began to slash and cut us with his sword! He was only cutting his own forgetfulness, I'm sure, for he loved us too much to wish us any harm. But he was so angry with himself that we got out of his way as fast as we could!

"Being ridden has been one of the consuming joys of my life. Especially being ridden to war!

"Of course I don't like unjust wars and I have tried never to carry cruel or evil riders. If I can, I throw them off! But, ah, there's nothing like a battle under a

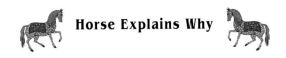

good fighter who is a just man! When dressed and decorated for war, with my chest armoured and my mane full of ribbons, I feel ready for anything!

"My brothers and I, with our riders, would wait for the signal to charge. Then would bound forward so swiftly that our hooves, as we flew over the rough ground, would strike sparks of fire from the stones. Snorting, neighing, we ran with all our might! Our riders would aim us towards the centre of the enemy and we would go, like one body, men and horses.

"Neigh! The wind against my skin!

"Neigh! The graceful, sure movement of the rider upon my back!

"Neigh! The shock and thrill when the two armies met, and we fought along with the men, with hooves and heads and teeth, thinking and acting as one, and then breaking away and charging again!

"I know pride is a dangerous feeling for those who want to be pure. But purity and pride are both in the nature of a horse. I have a small story to illustrate this.

"It is told from generation to generation among us that Ishmael was the one who trained the Arab horse. This is how he did it. He had me, and many of my brothers, among his horses. He treated us with great gentleness and kindness until the feeling of love was stirred in our hearts. We came to love this man more than our lives. He nursed us if we were ill or had scraped a knee or injured a hoof. He fed us with his own hands, especially on cold nights when we needed something extra for strength and encouragement. On hard rides he would walk over the rough places, to save our legs. If struggle and effort were required, he spared us as much as he could and we knew that he was striving just as hard as we were. We saw him sacrifice time and energy for us and we were prepared to do anything for him. When he called us with his special call, we competed with one another to reach him first.

"Then one day he kept us in our corral. We were brought no water. Naturally we became very thirsty, but we trusted that our master would take care of us. We waited all day, and at night went to sleep uncomfortable and puzzled.

"The next day also, we were left with no water. By now we were becoming miserable, and we could not understand why we were so neglected. However,

most of us still trusted our master. That night we spoke among ourselves and argued, some beginning to lose faith.

"The third day, our thirst was becoming unbearable. There was a river running not far away, and we could smell and hear the water. But try as we might, the fence was too high to leap, especially with our failing strength. We waited. At last our master came and, without a word, opened the gate wide so that we might run through. Out we streamed, with little in our minds but the compelling thought of drinking at last. When we had run about half way to the stream, suddenly, we heard his call. Some of us could not stand it, and ran on, soon to be knee-deep in the sweet running water. Others of us, and I am proud to include myself in their number, turned on our heels without even a thought of disobedience, and returned to our master. This was his test of our love.

"From us, those who returned, he bred the Arab horse. To love our masters in the face of suffering, to serve in the face of death – that is our creed. And I thank you."

"Thank *you*," mused Lion. "It was a pleasure, esteemed friend. It is rare to hear a story told in the old style, where the teller does not only dwell on himself, but gives us the history of his race and nation! On that high note, let us end today's meeting."

Big Fish
and the Man in the Storm

Big Fish knew that he had swallowed someone important but he did not know that it was the Prophet Jonah. He heard Jonah praying for forgiveness down in his belly, but he did not know that if Jonah had not done that, he might have stayed inside his belly until the end of time! I do not think Big Fish would have liked that very much, do you? Big Fish was then ordered to take Jonah right back to his people, and he did it. When the people found him, they knew they were witnessing a miracle, and they all took him back to town and listened carefully to his teachings. Of course Big Fish was far away in the sea by then.

Recording Angel

The animals were quite surprised to find, when they gathered the next morning, that it was raining. It was a refreshing, warm rain, gentle and light. It made the scents of the flowers and herbs even more wonderful than before, and the colours of the plants and leaves seemed to glow in the rainlight.

However, some of the animals did not want to get wet. The birds fluffed out their feathers and sought refuge under the leaves of the biggest trees. The cat-like animals put their ears and whiskers back and went up on the branches, not too close to the birds. The hoofed animals gathered together, heads bowed. Then Lion arrived.

"What's this?" he roared. "Rain? That's all very well for some of us, ducks and the like, but I don't want it to rain. We've been promised we can have anything we want here, so I want the rain to stop!"

The rain stopped immediately. Various ears, noses, and whiskers poked their

way out through the leaves, and gentle and curious eyes looked up to the sky. Blue, with scudding white clouds. "Now that's odd," said Dog, thinking aloud. "If we are only to have what we want, somebody must have wanted and wished for rain. Who was it?"

There was a splashing noise in the small pond, which the rain seemed to have filled to overflowing. In fact it was definitely larger than it had been before, and the flowers on its banks seemed to have moved back to encompass the greater amount of water. Fish poked his head up near the pond's edge beside some cat-tails and watercress. "It was I!" he spoke. His voice had a thin, wet sound like a small violin in the fog. "It was I! I love the patter of raindrops on my roof! I can look up and see the light moving out in widening circles, one after another, until I become quite giddy. And the water underneath becomes fresh and clean. It makes me feel all frisky and slithery. I want it to rain some more!"

So it began to rain, somewhat to the dismay of those animals who had begun their licking and shaking and preening in the new sunlight. Cow, who was always kind-hearted, asked with great presence of mind, "O please, please make it rain only on Fish's pond!" And so it was. A small cloud rained only over Fish, and everywhere else the sun shone.

"Fine, now that's attended to, shall we begin?" said Lion, finding a relatively dry spot and sitting down. It took some time for everyone to get settled and comfortable. Then the question was, who would be next? Once again, they heard the fine thin voice of Fish.

"I've caused so much commotion already that I may as well continue," he said. "I've a tale and a surprise. Which would you like first?"

"Surprise! Surprise!" shouted everybody at once.

"Very well," smiled Fish. "Here we go!" And he dived. For a few moments, the surface of the now large pond was broken only by raindrops and the ripples from Fish's tail. Then, as the animals watched, a great fin cut the water and a huge head arose and looked at them all, first with one eye, then with the other.

"Peace be with you," came the voice, which was like a bass viol to Fish's violin. "I'm glad I could join you." Fish poked his small head up nearby. "It's my big

brother!" he piped, "My big brother from the deep sea, who has agreed to join us for the morning! He really prefers the depths, you know, and it is quite unusual for him to come up or to speak at all. So, if it's all right with everybody, he'll tell his story now and dive down again."

"That's why the pond had to grow so large," he said as an afterthought.

The surface bubbled and the large head rose again.

"My story is not very long," Big Fish began. "But for me, it was the highlight of my life. I shall tell you. One time there was a storm. A storm at sea is a bit like my little brother's description of the rain. There are lights on the surface, and the water becomes fresher. But all the activity is up near the top. Deep down where I live, nothing ever changes. The deep currents move on, the deep life is as it always was. In the dim life down below the storm, one is only slightly aware of all that crashing and banging on the surface. We don't like it much. It's too busy and chaotic, if you understand me.

"During one such time, I was cruising at about 100 feet below the surface, somewhere off one of the African coasts, when I got a message from our Great Master to rise to the top. There was a really gigantic storm in progress. The waves were so high and the motion was so grand that I felt sure this was no ordinary gale or blow. This was a Divine Storm, and I was called up to be part of it. I saw a ship floundering in the waves. I don't know how it had stayed afloat; its masts were broken, and the water was rushing over its decks. People were on the ship, struggling to hold on to anything they could find, and a big group of them were gathered together at one side of the ship, causing it to dip dangerously. I had seldom seen people or had anything to do with them, so I swam closer to watch. They seemed to be having some kind of argument. That is, some were pulling one way and some another, all the time trying not to get washed overboard. One man in the middle caught my eye. The people were pulling at his garment but he freed himself and climbed to the side of the ship. He looked about for a moment and seemed to be praying. Then, he simply jumped. I was very surprised. I was sure that people can't swim very well, at least not from a fish's point of view, and that he would be killed by the rushing

water. I felt sorry for him, for he seemed to be a noble man, judging from the way he stood and held himself that moment before he jumped.

"Then a strange thing happened. I was ordered to swim to him, and to *swallow* him. I'm a shrimp eater. I had never eaten a man in my life, before or since. But I wasn't told to *eat* him exactly. I was told to swallow him and carry him to a certain place which I knew well by fish navigation. So, I did that. I opened my mouth very, very wide, and the sea carried him right in, and he didn't try to resist. I felt him go down my throat and into my belly. He was heavy and a little uncomfortable for me, especially when he turned over. However, I am so large that he didn't make much difference. I still kept feeling he must be someone special. Why else would he be saved from the storm like that?

"So I carried him, following my orders. The trip was short, only two or three days and nights. I don't know how he felt, down there in the dark in my belly. I'm sure he must have been hot and a little squished. I didn't eat anything while he was in there, and tried not to swallow much water. I came to the surface often and took in great gulps of air, hoping some would reach him. I knew he was alive because every now and then I would feel him move. And, very faintly, I could hear him praying. He kept saying the same thing over and over. I remember it still. He said, 'There is no God but You! Glory be to You; indeed, I have done wrong!'

"When I came near the place where I was to leave him, I waited for high tide. Then I swam in as close as I could get to shore. I tried to think of something I don't at all like to eat, giant squid I think it was, and then I just threw him up on the beach. He came out all white, like a little sand creature that has never been in the light. His clothes had all dissolved in my stomach – I couldn't control that – so he was bare skin like a crab with no shell. He just lay there half in and half out of the water, and I didn't know if he was alive or dead. I stayed near and watched him, and I saw him move a little. I trusted that he would make it if he didn't get cooked first. I told you he was all white, and it was a very sunny day.

"Then an odd thing happened. I had looked away for a minute, and when I looked back there was a big plant growing right next to him. I thought it grew

awfully fast, but I am not a specialist on earthly life forms. In a few minutes he was completely shaded by its broad leaves. I knew he was all right then and I swam away, for I was hungry.

"I couldn't forget him, though. Something about the way he jumped off the ship all by himself, and didn't fight when I swallowed him. I felt that he was under orders, just as I was, and that he had agreed to do what was necessary, just as I had. So I swam back the next day to check on him, and he was still lying there. There wasn't anything I could do for him, and I suppose he needed the rest. I went away.

"The next day I came again, and found him gone. There were a lot of footprints on the sand all around where the plant was growing. I could see them leading off in the direction of one of their living places. This looked like a big one, so I suppose there were many of his people there. They must have taken him home with them. I never saw him again.

"I swam back to the deep. My life continued as it had before. But I felt that I had been part of some amazing event, some grand order which I didn't fully understand. I hoped I had played my part honourably.

"Now, if you will excuse me, I've been over-long near the surface. There's a wonderful tunnel beneath here that takes me out to the great sea, and that is where I am going. Peace be with you." And he dived. The magnificent tail stood for an instant above the surface of the pond, and then disappeared. The animals watched in awe. None of them, except for Little Fish, had ever seen Big Fish before for more than a moment, or heard him speak at all. They felt very still and quiet, and few sounds were to be heard as they adjourned for that day.

Little Fish's Escape

Poor Little Fish did not have any idea that he was supposed to be lunch for the Prophet Moses and his young friend Joshua. He was riding along in a lunch basket. God had told Moses that he would find his teacher at the spot where he would lose the fish he planned to eat for lunch. So Moses probably expected the fish to disappear. But Moses fell asleep and Joshua forgot to tell him about Fish's escape until later. They went on their way, then they got hungry and ... no fish. Then Joshua remembered, and they retraced their steps to the rock and found the teacher Moses was looking for.

Recording Angel

The next day, bright and early, Little Fish greeted the group from his pond, which was back to its normal size. "My story is much less grand," he said, "as befits a little fish. However, it also involves one of those strange humans. And my human was like the man who jumped into the sea. He was somebody special. He was clearly different from the general school of people, and he knew it, too. I spent some time near him and heard him speak, so I know more about my man than Big Fish ever learned about his. I'll tell you.

"I was swimming about in the sea one day and had the misfortune to be caught in one of those nets the humans use to catch my kind. Struggle as I would, I could not get free, and only became more entangled in the net. So they pulled me up into a boat and unceremoniously dumped me on the hard floor. I jumped and flopped and gasped for breath and called for help, but none of my friends could help me, being all in the same condition as I. Soon I lost consciousness and soon after that I was dead.

"However, as we all know, the dead can still hear. Strangely, I could understand the talk of these humans. I do not know how. So I heard the fishermen talking about their 'catch', as they call us, and I heard myself counted among the others as they loaded us into baskets. We were all piled together, head to tail, but it didn't matter then because we were dead. They carried us somewhere and I know I passed hands, for I heard new voices speaking and they were different from the old. The sound of them was more musical and not so rough. I heard one voice, which was softer and gentler, say that I was a beautiful fish and good for her master. I remember thinking to myself that if I were going to be eaten, I would prefer to be eaten by that one with the gentle voice. But that was not to be.

"Other things happened to my body, I really can't tell you what, but after some time I found myself back in a basket. I was alone this time and wrapped up in something like a big leaf of seaweed. There were a few other things in the basket but I don't know about human food, so I don't know what they were. And I was beyond feeling, so I can't describe them to you.

"The basket was covered and then it was picked up by someone. It was carried, with me in it, for a long time. It was then that I heard their talk, for there were two of them.

"The one who was carrying me was named Joshua bin Nun. He carried me very carefully and he walked smoothly. His voice seemed younger than the voice of his companion. He spoke very respectfully to the older man, whom he called Moses.

"It seemed that Moses was a big teacher and a big speaker for his people. Even I could tell why, for his voice seemed to shake the basket when he spoke. Maybe it made Joshua shake too, I don't know. And it seemed that one of his people had asked him who, of all the people of the earth, knew the most. And Moses had answered, "I do." Now any guppy knows that no creature, fish or bird or human or otherwise, dare say they are the best or most of anything. That is very unwise. And quick as the flip of a flipper, our Lord made that clear to Moses.

"Right away God told Moses that there was another who had more knowledge than he. So of course Moses wanted to know how and where to meet him so he could learn from him. And God told him it would be at a place where two seas met. And at that place the fish would be lost.

"Naturally, on hearing this, I wondered about myself. How was I going to get lost out of a closed basket, wrapped as I was, and carried by this person Joshua? And how could I get lost since I was dead and couldn't move even the tip of my tail? But all things are possible, and I've heard many fishy stories. Anyway, I could do little else but wait.

"After some time, the two men stopped. I suppose they wanted to rest. We were near the sea; I could hear it sighing and breaking around the rock on which the men had placed the basket. After a while the older one stopped talking. I heard him breathing evenly and slowly the way big fish do when they're asleep. I don't know what the younger one was doing. Soon, I didn't care, for some remarkable things began to happen.

"First, I felt water on my skin. Water, after so long! I didn't stop to wonder how I could even feel anything. It was wonderful, and after it touched me, all of me came to life in a rush. I had so much energy that, without even thinking, I doubled over and gave a great leap, bursting out of my wrappers and out of the basket and into the light. I landed on stone. I have a passing memory of the younger man staring with his eyes popping out of his head like an octopus. I didn't care. I smelled water, I heard water, and I felt water, falling like rain on my scales and bringing life with it. I flopped again, and landed in it. It was fresh water, a spring. It was – how can I say ? – the *liveliest* water I have ever experienced. Fish become connoisseurs of water; we can sense every mineral, every trace of food or sound or temperature. This particular water was, for me, the carrier of life. It had bubbles of light and happiness in it. It was full of promise, and made me feel like a minnow again.

"As I sank beneath the surface, I was carried down a long, clear tunnel, straight away into the sea. And then I was home. I could scarcely believe what had happened, and just swam along lazily in the current for a while, moving my

flippers and swishing my tail and opening and shutting my gills. I wanted to be sure I was all there.

"After a time of pure happiness, I began to think again. And I wondered what had happened to the two men. I bore them no ill-will, it is a fish's life to eat and be eaten, but I did wonder about their story and who would come when I got lost. The older man had seemed so wise that I really wanted to see who could be wiser. So I turned on my tail and swam back the way I had come, seeing an area of quiet water from which I could observe the rock. I found a small inlet and poked my head out. There I saw an amazing sight.

" Two men were just hurrying out to the rock from a road that passed nearby. They were coming fast and one was carrying a basket. I guessed they were the two who had me before. Why they left the rock and returned, I can't tell you because I don't know. Then I saw a third person. He was dressed all in green, from top to bottom. He asked them who they were and they introduced themselves. This must have been the one they were looking for. They all went off together.

"I hope Moses learned something. It is a great honour to find a wise teacher. Big Fish has been that for me, although I don't see him often. And that is my story. Thank you for listening."

There was a sudden squawk and Seagull flew down beside Lion. "I think I know some more of Fish's story!" she said with excitement. "I know what happened next! Please, Fish, Lion, may I tell?"

Before they had a chance to answer, Seagull went on. "I was nearby that day when you came back to life, Fish. I saw you whoosh into the water. I didn't know what else was going on, but I saw the men too. The ones who were carrying you and the other one, the green one.

"After you swam away, the young one sat very still. Then the old one woke up, and they picked up the basket and moved on. I flew around a bit, fishing – uh, excuse me – and after a while I saw the two men come back. Suddenly I saw there in the water, or on the water, it was a little hard to tell, this man all in green. They spoke together but I was a little out of earshot. In order to hear

them, I flew down to the water and dipped my beak into the sea. Then I heard the green man say, 'Do you see that bird in the water? Compared to God's Knowledge, my knowledge and your knowledge are as tiny as the amount of water this bird has taken with its beak from the sea.' Then they moved off together.

"I thought about that quite a long time. I couldn't see that I'd had any effect on the sea at all. Fish was gone, and the men were gone, so I flew away."

Fish thanked Seagull for adding to his story, and disappeared beneath the water. "It's odd," said Ant quite suddenly, "how many of us have died and come back to life again. I myself saved my people from dying. I wonder if I should have left them alone just for the pleasure of witnessing their rebirth?"

"We'll hear about it tomorrow," said Lion with one of his great yawns. "Right now, I'm feeling quite kittenish..." and he did a back flip off his rock and pounced on Wolf, who had been dozing in the sunlight and had missed the end of Fish's story. The two raced off over the hill, leaving the others laughing and rather relieved that Lion hadn't pounced on *them*.

The Very Brave Ant

Ant's story is quite clear. Solomon loved hearing that small voice, and it made him so happy that he really did stop his whole huge army to save the ant-hill, and he thanked God for giving him the gift of understanding the language of animals.

Recording Angel

Ant sat on top of her ant-hill and all the animals came around as close as they could get so as to hear her. As it turned out, her voice was quite shrill and it carried a long distance. "My story concerns the Prophet Solomon and the safety of my people," said Ant.

"All of us know about Solomon. He was the only human who really understood us, or at least, understood our speech. He understood the birds, and the fish, the amphibians and the animals and the insects and the jinn. God gave him this gift and he was very happy to have it. He used to listen to us all and to speak with us from time to time. He did have his lapses, as Horse has pointed out, but he was always sorry for them. But I don't need to tell you this.

"On the day I'm speaking of, Solomon had gathered together his armies. He had an army of people, an army of jinn, and an army of birds. They made a great show all lined up and marching together. Of course the birds didn't march, they flew in formation overhead. I don't know where they were going or why. I think Solomon liked to take them out on drill sometimes, just for the pleasure of it. Any ant can understand that. We are raised in a military manner, and are accustomed to obeying orders and acting in units large and small. We think better as a group than as individuals. There is no one more lost and confused

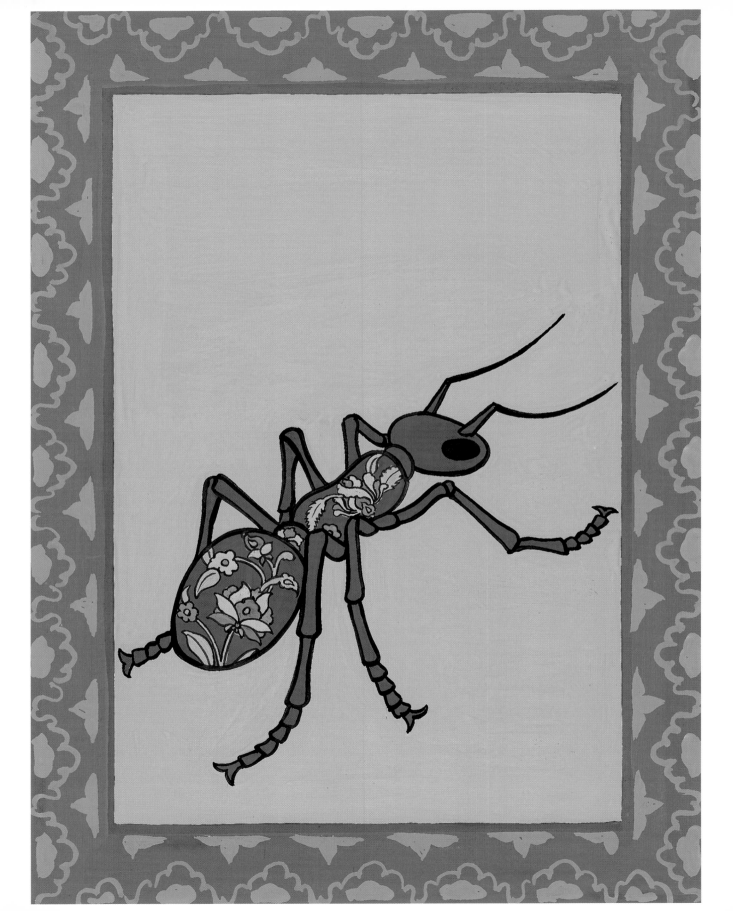

than an ant without his or her tribe, and we go to great lengths to take care of one another. Which introduces my story.

"While that magnificent army was preparing to march, all we ants were going about our business – we are always very busy – seeking and finding and carrying and hauling and so on. We were clearing our runways of landslides. We were building new exits and entrances. Some of us were hauling rocks out of the way and others were taking them up and out and dropping them over the sides of the hill. Some were searching for food and sending messages back when they found some. Big groups were going out to bring it home. Some were pulling dead bees out of the road. It was a typical day in the ant world.

"I happened to be sitting on top of the hill, much as I am now, as I was on guard duty. I was looking sharply about, watching the sky and earth for birds and large insects. At the same time I was sensing the ground for vibrations and movement. I started to notice a rhythmic beating. It was quite far away at first. I kept listening and sensing with my feelers and my feet. The beating grew louder. It was coming nearer. Closer it came and closer, until the whole ant-hill was shaking! Then, in the distance, I perceived the first ranks of the soldiers of Solomon. They were heading straight for us! I knew it was his army because of the strange forms of the jinn and all the birds flying overhead. It spelled nothing but danger for us!

"I went into action fast! I started yelling at the top of my lungs, 'Alarm, alarm! O Ants! O Ants! Enter your houses, lest Solomon and his armies crush you! They won't even notice you are here!'

"I dashed around my post, calling and shouting and beating my feet. Ants came up from below and I transferred the message to them through our feelers. They ran off to do their duty. The whole hill sprang into action. All work was stopped. I felt proud of the splendid discipline of the ants: captains ordered their troops, workers formed tidy rows, and the stragglers were encouraged to hurry.

"While all this was going on, the great booming of thousands of marching feet was coming closer and closer. I looked up and saw Solomon at the head of his army! He was very grand on his powerful horse. I understand now exactly what friend Horse is talking about when he speaks of the union of horse and rider. But I was much too busy to think about such things then. Solomon looked like a moving mountain to me, and he was coming right towards my home! I was terrified for my people...houses can be rebuilt with simple effort, but the poor ants! So many would be crushed...

"I called and called again, trying to be sure that every one of us had heard. I was ready to sacrifice my life – what is one life when the hill is in danger? – when I looked again and saw that the giant man and horse had stopped! Nearly all the ants were inside. I hoped they had gone far down, for a horse's hoof can utterly destroy the top of a hill. However, we have deep tunnels for such emergencies. The guard's entrance was near me. I took one last look before diving down it, and I saw an amazing thing.

"It was so amazing I did a somersault, stopped my dive, and looked again! The earth was still shaking, but for another reason! The great prophet, the great king, the great Solomon was laughing!

"Even ants, for all our discipline, have curiosity. I couldn't imagine, from my state of terror and alarm, why he was laughing! The horse was still. So I listened. Solomon was very joyful. He was praying! He was thanking God for all the gifts he and his parents had received. He was asking God to remind him always to be grateful. He was asking guidance to do what is right, and he wanted to be included among God's good servants. Can you imagine, He wanted to be a servant? From an ant's point of view, service is everything. My estimation of this man grew higher and higher. He had understood my call and actually done something about our danger. He had done what was right: he stopped that huge horse in time. He had a sense of humour: I wasn't sure what was funny, but I liked his laugh. And he understood about service. So I liked him. I still like him".

Suddenly Ant became very flustered and disappeared down her hole. Horse chuckled. "Such a noble creature!" he said. "So brave! I shall try to watch my hoofs more carefully from now on. It may not be so difficult here. One is so much more aware of everything....Neigh....!"

Hoopoe, the Spy

As I said, there are many stories about Solomon. Hoopoe tells one of them. Hoopoe is a wise bird, but Solomon is known for having the greatest wisdom of anybody. Certainly he was wiser than the Queen of Sheba. She thought that her real throne was fake, and she thought that the fake water was real. She was so bewildered that she gave up, and followed Solomon's teaching. That was wise of her, too. I am not sure if Hoopoe ever did figure it out, I must go and explain it to him.

Recording Angel

Hoopoe flew down and settled beside Lion. His eyes darted this way and that as he quickly counted the animals and found them all to be present. "Please excuse me for counting; it is always my custom since the days of the Prophet Solomon. He was always aware of who was where. He had tremendous powers of observation. I stayed as close to him as I could, and became one of his messengers and scouts. Thus I was able to observe him and learn from him.

"He was quite an amazing man, as you can imagine, having all the languages of creation moving in his mind at once. His court was filled with every kind of bird and beast, man and jinn. He wanted to share in the special knowledge of each. From the jinn he learned about many of the strange powers of their world, like walking through walls and moving like smoke. From us birds he learned about far lands and high mountains that humans were unable to reach, being bound to earth as they then were. We used to delight in bringing him news of distant places. He was always very attentive when anyone knew something he didn't know; he would listen closely and remember everything. That was why he

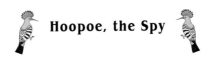

was such a good and powerful king. He paid attention.

"But he was a tough one, I have to say. He demanded, and received, absolute obedience from his subjects. He gave a lot and expected a lot back in return. Beware if one tried to fool him or cheat him in any way. And he expected everyone to be present when he wanted them.

"One day he was holding court as usual, and for some reason he looked for me. Alas, I was not there, for I was off on one of my journeys to gather information, and I had found a new land and a new people. I was quite involved in observing them, and I forgot the time.

"Solomon was *not* pleased. He wanted me, and I was not there. He asked the people around him where the hoopoe was. He wondered whether I could possibly be absent from his court. Then he said that he was going to punish me severely or even kill me if I did not have a good excuse! He was that kind of king. You had to keep on your toes around him! He wouldn't really have killed me, but his displeasure was as hard as death.

"So when I flew in- I wasn't very late in fact- I had to make my explanations. I felt terrible for displeasing him but, happily, I had a wonderful excuse. I was quite proud of myself, in fact. I had discovered something this time that I was sure he didn't know. I said:

"O my King, I have found out something that you do not know. I come to you from Sheba with real news.

"I found a woman there ruling over them. She is a strong and wise queen, and she has many wonderful things, among them a magnificent throne. But I found her and her people worshipping the sun instead of God!

"I was truly amazed and horrified by this. Here were people who had obviously been blessed by God. They had nice houses, lovely clothes and delicious food, a good government and a fine queen. I couldn't understand how on earth they could fail to be grateful and thankful to the One who gave them everything. But as I watched them, they bowed down to the sun. Their worship was very complicated, with priests and robes and pictures and temples and everything like that. It is true that the sun has power, but it's not God!

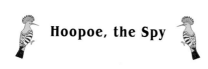

"I was becoming very indignant and critical of those people, when Solomon spoke. I think he was still angry with me for being late. He said, 'We shall see whether you have told the truth or are one of the liars! Here's a letter from me. Go and take it to them, drop it and then perch somewhere nearby and wait to see what answer they give in return.'

"I was happy to do that. It was a long flight, but I would have done anything to stop his being angry with me! Also I hoped he would help those people. So I flew back to Sheba and in through an open window and dropped the letter at the queen's feet. She was surprised, I can tell you! But, being a queen, she quickly regained her composure, and opened the letter which had been picked up by a courtier and handed to her.

"After she finished reading, she looked up and said to the people who surrounded her (I forgot to say that there were a lot of people around her just as there were a lot around Solomon, except hers were only humans), 'O you chieftains! A truly noble letter has been brought to me. Listen. It is from Solomon, and it says: 'In the name of God, the Most Compassionate, the Merciful. God says, do not raise yourselves up against Me, but come to Me in willing surrender!'

"That was all there was in the letter. The queen looked around at her chiefs and advisers and said, 'O you chieftains! Give me your opinion on the problem with which I am now faced. I would never make an important decision without your advice.'

"The chiefs considered only a moment, and then they said to her, 'We are powerful lords and mighty warriors in battle. However, it is for you to command. You decide.' I was listening from my perch on a great beam overhead. I couldn't tell from their voices if they were just being polite and formal, or if they really didn't know what to do. Obviously, they respected and honoured their queen. I thought to myself, 'She must be an exceptional woman.' Then I went on listening.

"The queen spoke again. 'It is true that kings, when they enter a place, ruin it, and they shame the noblest people. This is the way they always behave. I have

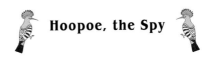

decided to send a present to Solomon, and wait to see with what answer the messengers return.'

"That was all I needed to know. Swiftly, I flew back to my king and reported what I had overheard. So he was completely prepared for the messengers of the queen when, some days later, they arrived bearing rich gifts.

"My king greeted the queen's embassy while seated in his magnificent courtroom, surrounded by his court of beasts, jinn and men, in their gorgeous clothing, fur, and plumage. He was the picture of power and might. The ambassador stood before him and Solomon said, 'Do you people mean to add to my wealth? But that which God has given me is better than all he has given you! No, it is only you yourselves who rejoice in this gift of yours!'

"I imagined the ambassador was crestfallen at the rejection of his gift. But he needed only to look around to see that it was true: God had blessed Solomon with every earthly treasure. Besides that, he had given him great wisdom. So what could the queen's man say?

"Solomon continued, 'Go back to your people. We shall definitely come to them with forces which they will never be able to withstand. We shall most certainly drive them out of that land, disgraced and humbled!'

"The ambassador left, and I wondered what would happen next. Were we to have war? I didn't think so. Solomon didn't want to kill people, he wanted them to understand. So I listened to what went on, and watched closely to see what would happen.

"Solomon learned by his intelligence that the queen, as he expected, was coming to him. He turned to his council. 'O nobles and chiefs,' he said, 'Which of you can bring me her throne before she and her followers come to me in surrender to God?'

"Quickly one of the big jinn – they are called Ifrits – spoke up. 'I'll bring it to you,' he said, 'before you can rise from your seat! I'm strong enough to do it, and I can be trusted!'

"But there was among the council members a man who was truly an enlightened being. He had deep understanding of everything from God. He said

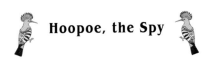

quietly, 'I will bring it to you within the twinkling of an eye,' and he did it! I was so excited I was hopping up and down on my perch above their heads. 'How did he do that?' I asked. But I had no time to wonder, because my king was speaking. He was truly grateful to have such men around him, and he thanked God. Then he asked the same man to transform the throne beyond recognition. He planned to test the queen, to see if she could recognise the truth or not. Her mother and father and ancestors had no faith. They couldn't see the truth in front of their eyes. Could she? The transformed throne was incredibly beautiful, but on the surface it didn't look like the old one at all.

"At last the queen and her company arrived, and were greeted as kings greet queens. Then she was asked, 'Is this your throne?'

"She answered, 'It is as though it were the same!' My master was very happy at her words. They meant that she could recognise the truth under the disguise. So he tried another test. She was invited to enter the court.

"Now this courtroom had a floor of polished glass. It was smoother than any floor you've ever seen, smoother than the inside of an eggshell, smoother than a mother's beak. And it was shiny, so it really looked like water, like a mirage in the desert. So when the queen came to the door, she thought she had to wade across a lake! She tucked up her skirts to do it, when Solomon said, 'This is only a palace paved with slabs of glass.'

"She looked at him. She realised she had been mixing everything up. She gave up and saw that God knew all the mysteries she could never know. In those moments of the tests she surrendered to the will of God. My master had succeeded in confusing her so much that she became unconfused. Isn't that amazing? So she and all her people gave up worshipping the sun. I don't know what they did with all those temples and things. Perhaps they turned them into schools or barns or something. The queen stayed for some days among us. A big party was given with a lot of entertainment and everybody rejoiced.

"But I spent many nights sitting in the rafters or outside in the branches of the great trees, trying to puzzle it out. How did she know it was her throne? It didn't *look* like her throne. Maybe it *felt* like her throne. And if she was so clever, why

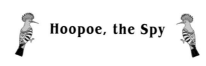

didn't she see that the floor was glass? And, when she saw that she didn't see, how did that make her know God? How did Solomon know what to do? At last I thought, Hoopoe, you are a bird. You do not have the mind of Solomon. Let it go. But now that we are here, as soon as I get the chance, I intend to go and ask him, politely, to explain it to me. And that is my story."

For a long time after Hoopoe finished, the animals stayed around discussing what had happened to the queen of Sheba. Finally the snake, who had been quite quiet throughout the discussion, spoke softly. "I have sssome experience in things being not what they ssseem," he hissed. "So I shall speak tomorrow." Then he slithered away.

Snake
Comes to Life

The Egyptians had made slaves of the Family of Israel, so God ordered Moses and his brother Aaron to rescue them. He gave Moses some special miracles. One of them was to change his staff into a real snake and back again. The Egyptians loved magic, and they were very good at it. But Moses' miracle out-magicked even the magicians.

Recording Angel

Snake slithered slowly out from under Lion's rock, and composed himself in a coil in the warm sun. The smaller mammals, such as Mouse and Mole, placed themselves at some distance away, even though they knew it was safe in the Garden. Old habits die hard. The others sat very quietly so as not to miss a syllable of Snake's softly hissed story.

"Most of my kind are born from eggs, grow, live and die like many other creatures. I have a different tale, a curious one, so come closer, come clossser, and listen," he said.

No one moved very much, but they all pricked up their ears and the meeting place became even more silent. Snake's tongue went in and out a few times and the tip of his tail twitched.

"I, whom you see before you, was not always a sssnake," he whispered. "Strange, ssstrange, once I was a stick, a ssstaff of wood. These shining ssscales, this sssslippery tail, this sssilvery head, these yellow eyes...were nothing but a shepherd's ssstaff...a sssimple shepherd's ssstaff, sssssso....." and Snake uncoiled and lay out long and flat on the ground. Suddenly he appeared to be a stick of wood, so much so that the animals rubbed their eyes in disbelief.

"Sssee, sssee," he said, recoiling into a series of compact loops, "what God made of me in the hands of hisss prophet Mosesss? What you just sssaw was what ssstupified and confounded the magiciansss of the pharaoh, the sssingle sssovereign of ancient Egypt!" He flicked his tongue in and out.

"My massster Moses, was living and studying with his teacher in the desssert near Sssinai. He had his family and his sssheep with him. He sssaw a light in the desssert far off. He went to sssee who or what it was. He thought he might find other people, and from them sssseek directions, or hear a ssstory, or discover some newsss. He went to find fire. He went for all these reasssons, and I know, for I went with him. At that time I was only a ssstaff, a ssstaff used to lean on, a ssstaff used to beat down leavesss for the sssheep, a ssstaff used for other reasssons. I know becausss I heard my massster Mosesss explain what happened to hisss brother Aaron, who needed to undersssstand.

"My massster Moses came to the place where the light was, and he heard a voice, the voice of God, ssspeaking to him (here Snake began to shiver slightly). The voice of God ssspeaking in the wildernesss is sssomething to hear, and He told my massster Mosesss to take off his ssshoes! 'Thisss isss the Sssacred Valley of Tuwa!' I think thessse were the firssst wordsss I ever heard, asss the life began ssstirring in me. I was ssstill a ssstaff, but now I was a ssstaff in the presssence of God...

"God asked my massster what he held in his hand and Moses told him I was his ssstaff. God told my massster to throw me down on the ground, and he did. Sssuddenly I came to life, writhing, twisting, ssslithering life, ssssliding so ssswiftly that my massster was ssscared and sssought to run away! But God told him not to be afraid! He said, 'The messsage bearers need have no fear in My presssence!'

"Then God made me a ssstaff once again. But I remembered. I remembered and I ssstill remember. And when my massster Moses needed me to come once again to life, I was ready.

"He carried me with him to Egypt, where he went with hisss brother Aaron, Egypt is a land where my ancessstors were highly honoured, an ancient place

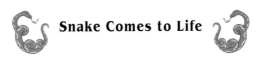

where both the sssnake and the ssstaff were known to be the sssigns of a god. We went to the Pharaoh's palace and my massster Moses challenged him to ssset free the Family of Isssrael, who were enssslaved there in Egypt. Pharaoh thought he could do anything. He was proud, proud, was he. He and my massster agreed to a show of power before the people. Hisss magiciansss againsst usss.

"It was a great feasssst day. We met near the mighty river Nile. The light was sssparkling on the water, and the people were dresssed for a holiday in white, and red, and gold. They were waiting in expectation of the great event! All the magiciansss had sssilvery robes and ssstrange hats. They alssso had their ropesss and their ssstaffssss. I sensssed one after another for life. Nothing. Then they were asssking my massster who should throw firssst and he sssaid, 'You throw!' Ssso they threw. For an inssstant I thought their ssstafffs were alive! SSSSSSS! But they were fooling, fooling the people, there wasss no true life in them! Then Moses threw me! Praise God! I flew from the hand of the prophet and fell to earth sssswirling, twisssting, darting. I sssswallowed them one after the other. Foul Fakesss! Foolsss!"

Snake stopped for breath. His head was darting this way and that and the animals were following his every movement.

"Sssuch a fine day," he continued, "Sssuch a grand disssplay of the colours and the formsss and the magic of Egypt! There by the rivvver, the great rivvver, with all the people watching, and the proud Pharaoh watching me sssswallow the fake magic of his magiciansss...and he wasss horrified, mortified, defeated, degraded, disssgraced! Nobody knows the diffference between the true and the falsssse like a magician. Ssso, when they sssaw me devour their ropesss and their ssstafsss, they fell down on the ground! They cried out, 'We believe in the Sssussstainer of all the worldsss, the Ssssussstainer of Moses and Aaron!'

"Pharaoh was furiousss! He threatened them with horrible punisssshment and death. They didn't care. They were convinced. They had ssseen the Truth and were finissshed with their falsssse, fake magic!

"I returned to the hand of my massster. My work was finissshed. Asss his ssstaff I ssserved him for many more yearsss asss he sssaved the Family of

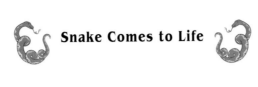

Isssrael, crosssed the sssea, and returned to the desssert. Ssssssssss, the desssert, my home, my sssun..."

Snake went off into a sort of dream, and all the animals went with him, seeing the Sinai, the sun, the stillness, the land of Moses. They saw the towering mount, they felt the awesome presence of...

Hoopoe, always the observer, coughed slightly. It was enough. They woke up, as if they had been in a dream of mystery and magic. They looked around, wondering. Snake lay asleep in the sunlight. The stillness was broken by the call of one of the birds. Somebody moved. There was the flash of Fish's tail in the pond. Nobody felt much like talking. After a while most of them got up and wandered off to other parts of the Garden.

Raven opened his great beak. "I shall speak tomorrow," he said seriously. "I have a brief story which will bring this gathering back to earth."

"But we're not on earth," said Cow. "We're in Paradise!"

"I know," said Raven, "but you know what I mean."

Frog and Grasshopper Speak Up

Grasshopper and Frog tell you what happened after Snake's story ended. God sent all sorts of punishments on the Egyptians because Pharaoh would not keep his promise to Moses. One of these punishments was a plague of frogs, and another of locusts. Grasshopper tells the locust story because they are close relatives and do the same business in life, and locusts do not talk as well!

Recording Angel

The next day the dignified Raven arrived prepared to speak, but he found that two others had preceded him. Frog and Grasshopper were sitting side by side in the middle of the circle, and they had already started talking. Cow whispered to him that they knew some more of Snake's story and had asked to finish it. So Raven stood aside politely and listened.

"...was furious, and he wouldn't listen to anybody," croaked Frog in an excited voice. "He put them off and put them off, and refused to let the Family of Israel free. He was so sure that he was so great he just couldn't believe that Moses had it in him to do any more. He didn't believe in God, you know. So he thought it was him against Moses. But he was wrong, wrong, wrong! Ho ho!" And Frog made three enormous leaps around the circle before taking his place once again.

"You see!" piped up Grasshopper. "Pharaoh thought HE was a god! He thought HE would live forever! He thought HE could do anything he liked! By my legs and music, he was wrong, wrong, wrong!"

Frog was smiling a big froggy smile. "God is so Great," he croaked, "that He didn't need to use anything very big to punish Pharaoh. He didn't use

mountains or winds and he didn't use the sea until the very end. He used little beings, bacteria, and us!" Frog leaped straight up in the air and landed beside Lion. "Us, sir, we little people. We have a thing or two to say! He used us to bother those Egyptians until they were fair out of their minds! He used us to bite 'em, and slither 'em, and nibble 'em, and distress 'em until they were begging for mercy, they were indeed!"

"I hopped in Pharaoh's soup!" shouted Frog. "I splashed him and sloshed him and hopped away leaving frogprints all over his nice white linen tablecloth! I jumped in his wife's bed! I jumped on her head! I scared all the children and went in the kitchen and hopped, hopped, hopped in the bread!'

"I, too," said Grasshopper, "made their lives miserable. My family and I flew into their houses and over their roof-tops and moved into their gardens and fields and barns. We ate up the tender green shoots of wheat and the lovely silver heads of barley and the sweet wet leaves of alfalfa and the vegetables, oh, the vegetables! We ate up the grain, stored and otherwise, and they had no food, food, food!"

"Oh yes," croaked Frog joyously, "There was never a time, before or since, when my people and I had such fun! They opened the sugar bowl and I popped out my head! I hid in their slippers under the bed! I swam in their water-bottles – ah, the cool water! – and spoiled their baths! I put holes in the papyrus and warned all the fish to keep out of their nets and..."

"And before you even came," chirped Grasshopper, "we had eaten up nearly everything to the point that they had nothing left but straw! But they were still stubborn. Every time any of us obeyed our orders and made life impossible for them, they would say to Pharaoh, 'Help!' and he would say to Moses, 'All right, you win, tell your God to stop it and we'll let your people go, go, go!'

"But!" croaked Frog angrily, "As soon as Moses asked God to put a stop to it, and we were told to quit, there they would be again, ill-treating the Children of Israel as if nothing had ever happened! What a stubborn and thankless lot they were. Of course I think it was mainly the Pharaoh and his priests and nobles who were to blame, while their people were suffering, but who knows? I did

what I was told, and my people had a good time. Pharaoh did finally give up, though."

"Yes!" said Grasshopper. "I watched it all happen! I was gnawing on some grain in the store-rooms of the royal palace on the day that Pharaoh finally sent for Moses. I sneaked into the throne room on the back of a servant and was never noticed. Pharaoh told him that he was going to set the people free. He had a scowl on his face and no good in his heart when he said it. 'Git out, the ruddy lot a'yer, and don't let me see yer faces agin,' was the way he sounded, although they put it all in official language for the record."

"My cousin told me what happened after that!" said Frog. "The Children of Israel prepared to go. They packed all their bags and boxes and stuff. They got their clothes and necklaces and bracelets and rings and paint pots and hairpins and sandals and loincloths and robes and hats and wigs and make-up and cooking pots and dishes and trays and tools and..."

Grasshopper picked up the tale. "And they loaded their donkeys and camels and oxen with all this stuff very fast because Moses was urging them to hurry, and off they went in a big parade across the desert towards the sea!"

"And you can believe that Pharaoh was ANGRY," shouted Frog, "and he told his generals and armies to go after them and bring them back! He broke his promise AGAIN!"

"Yes, yes, yes," sawed Grasshopper, rubbing his legs together furiously, "and they raced on towards the sea. Moses knew just what he was doing, but nobody else did, and the armies of Pharaoh were coming up fast behind. They had discipline and speed, and the Children of Israel were just straggling along with their babies and their baggage. But they had their prophet, and Moses was following God's orders and never wavered."

"They got to the sea!" croaked Frog.

"And Moses hit it with his staff!" shouted Grasshopper.

"And the sea OPENED!" yelled Frog!

"And the people went across, they did, they did, they did," sighed Grasshopper, exhausted.

"Except for the army following them," crooned Frog. "Pharaoh was at the head of it, in all his splendid armour with banners on either side, full of confidence and proud as ever. He led his army right up to the edge of the sea, and the waters were still pulled back in great walls on either side. Then he did a funny thing. I can't understand it. No reasonable frog would have done it. The Children of Israel walked across the sea floor, but they really had no other choice, and their prophet promised them it was all right. But why would Pharaoh follow them? Why? There were the two great walls of water, quivering and shimmering, and full of fish and eels and seaweed and shells and octopi and who knows what else. They were held apart by what? How? Only God could do that. Pharaoh simply could not have believed he could do that."

"But he must have thought he was so great that the sea would stay open for him too," sighed Grasshopper. "Poor Pharaoh, not to mention his army. All wet, they were, all wet, wet, wet." Grasshopper pretended to shed a tear and rubbed a sorrowful note with his legs.

"Nothing wrong with wet!" said Frog. "Nothing wrong with wet!" He jumped into the pond, surprising Fish, and swam around in lazy circles.

"There was another of us," mused Grasshopper. "It was Louse. She was sent too. She made the Egyptians very unhappy and scratchy. But when I asked her to come today, she refused. She said she was busy doing something with Flea, and anyway, she said that she had seen so much of all of us on earth that she wanted some time off. But she sent her regards.'

"Those regards I can do without," said Dog aside to Camel.

"So can I," croaked Raven. "I'll speak tomorrow. This has been quite enough excitement for one day." And he flapped away.

Raven is Serious

God sent Raven down to the ground to show Adam's son Cain how to bury his brother Abel. It was a sad thing. Animals have a hard time understanding murder, because few of them ever kill their own kind. But they have learned that people are different.

Recording Angel

The raven walked up and down soberly before them in his black suit. He seemed very dignified except for a certain rakishness to his feathers, which were continually ruffling out of place, no matter how much he tried to keep them stiff and proper. Also there was a clever brilliance to his yellow eyes, as he turned his head first this way and then that to peer at the company. When he spoke, his voice rather resembled a cross between a croak and a cry. He had a sad story, for which his voice was fitting. He began:

"This is a tale from the beginning of time. I do not mean the beginning of all time, but of the time recorded by humans and passed down in their words. We, the nation of ravens, were watching when the first humans began to move upon the earth. We were interested in these strange creatures who had neither beaks nor claws, but who seemed able to make things to serve the same purposes. They could not dig well with their hands, but they could dig a hole with a stick or a shoulder bone. They could not crack large nuts with their teeth, but they could crack them between two stones. They had neither fur nor feathers, but they kept warm with the coats of others. Strange people; we watched them.

"Many children were born to the father and the mother of these people. They

took a long, long time to become adult. I had watched generation after generation of eggs become chicks become fledglings become full-grown ravens before the children of the people had ever left the nest.

"Among these children were two sons. They grew up together, and I watched them as they grew strong and developed into adults, whom they call men. These sons worked on the land and in the forests. As I made my daily flights, I would see them here and there, cutting, planting, hunting. They had skills we ravens have not. But they could not fly, and there were many things they could not see. They could not see the silver fish in the middle of the streams. They could not see the best perches at the tops of trees. They were also very young in the world, and there were things they did not know. We ravens are an older race than they.

"I watched the two young men as they prepared to make some kind of prayer. I did not know what they were doing exactly, because it was not something ravens do. But I knew it was a prayer because of the way they went about it. Quietly and seriously, they each went out alone and gathered certain things. Then they each went to a special place and put their things there on a raised spot. Then they moved back and made certain motions in a certain order, which I had seen them make before.

"I really wanted to understand what they were doing, so I settled myself on a large branch in a nearby tree, and paid attention. The men were waiting. I looked at their piles of things, and all at once one of them began to glow. It became lighter and lighter, like the light of early morning. Pretty soon every bit of it was glowing and shining with the most wonderful light I had ever seen. The younger brother, whose pile it was, became filled with light also and his face was bright with love.

"The older brother, however, became darker and darker. His pile was not touched by the wonderful light, nor was his being. Instead of love showing on his face, there was anger and fury. He looked the way a raven looks when a hawk has unexpectedly taken his prey out from under his beak.

"After a while, the light faded and the brothers began to speak. I hopped down to a lower limb in order to hear them clearly. The older one, the one who was

angry, was speaking in a loud and terrible voice. He was saying, 'Be sure I will kill you!'

"The younger one, still filled with light, replied to his big brother, 'Surely, God accepts only from those who are conscious of Him.'

"The elder one advanced on the younger, the way birds do when they are fighting over a female. But the younger one did not move and did not even raise his voice. I was amazed by this. Why didn't he defend himself or fly away? He just kept talking. He said, 'Even if you lay your hands on me to kill me, I will not lay my hands on you to kill you. I fear God. If you kill me you have to take on all my bad deeds as your own. If you want to take on all my sins as well as all your sins, go ahead! But then you'll end up in Hell!'

"The elder brother was very excited and very angry. The more the younger talked, the more angry he became, until, oh horrors, he did lift up his hands and kill his brother. It was a terrible thing to see. Ravens do not kill one another. Tigers, bears, cows, horses – no animals kill their own kind. Apparently people are something different. This was the first of many, many murders by man.

"Everything stopped. Time stood still. There was no sound of bird or beast or insect. The wind dropped. A cloud went over the sun. The elder brother stood looking at what he had done, and his face was terrible to see.

"After a while, he began to move about, but he didn't seem to know what to do. His brother was lying there on the ground. He should have been covered up. It was wrong for him to be lying there. Time passed. Nothing happened. The man didn't do anything but stand there looking blank. Finally, I myself could not stand it any longer. These ignorant people!

"I flapped down to earth near the dead brother where I knew the other one could see me. I began to scratch in the earth with my strong claws, making a shallow hole. I was trying to tell him something and I knew he was watching. After a while I flew up to a nearby branch and waited.

"The man said out loud, 'Oh, woe is me! Am I then too weak to do what this raven did, and to hide the nakedness of my brother's body?'

"He then felt deeply ashamed and sorry for what he had done. He dug a deep

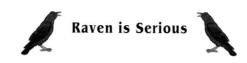

hole and buried his brother in it, covered it over and went away. I don't know what became of him.

"I'm sorry to darken even a moment of Paradise with this story. But our aim is to know and to understand. Perhaps one of you will understand that event better than I did. Thank you."

Raven sat down. Nobody said anything. Most of them, at one time or another, had seen both good and bad in the way humans behaved on earth. They knew that people could be like Dog's master, and could be like the elder brother in Raven's story. They could be light or dark and lots of shades in between. They shrugged, shook, and got up. All that was over now. "I'll be next," said Camel.

Camel's Sandy Spot

Camel tells a story about Salih and the people of Thamud. They were very proud and the rich ones were very selfish. They did not want to share their water with God's camel, and they did not want the poor people to get free milk, either.

Recording Angel

For some reason a sandy spot had appeared in the middle of the circle. Camel was walking around and around in it, delighted. As she stepped, her soft feet spread out on the sand like pillows. They made no sound at all, nor did Camel herself. Her eyes, which had two rows of thick blond eyelashes, were closed. Her mouth, which was always smiling anyway, looked even more pleased than usual. Her tail, which hung down like a bell-pull, was almost wagging, and her lovely fur was glowing in the soft heavenly light.

It was so pleasant to watch someone having such a good time, that nobody said anything for a while. At last Camel opened her eyes and looked around dreamily. "It's my turn, isn't it?" she said.

"I suppose you noticed my small parade in the sand, here. I can't tell you how wonderful this sand is. It's very soft but it holds you up well, and it's cool. Can you imagine – here we are, the sun is shining – and it's cool! Never have I felt such sand! I think I'm going to ask for a special bed of it over there by the Lote-tree. When I came here I was so happy with all the green and grass that I vowed I never wanted to see, smell, or feel sand again. Yes, Hoopoe, you *can* smell sand, or sandy places, at least. It's a dry, clear smell usually. But He knows us better than we know ourselves, I guess, and He knew I missed it, so here's my sand. Oh joy. Look how it squishes out around the edges of my foot pads. How lovely.

"And now my story. Humans have always found a lot of uses for me. I shall list them. One, they think I'm beautiful. They love to watch me run; they love to see me alone or in groups; they love to see my colours; and to count me, even. Two, I let them ride on me. I complain sometimes, it is true, but I do let them. Three, I let them put enormous loads on my back and I carry them, more or less willingly, wherever they want me to go. Four, they love my milk. I'm told they make things with it, though why I can't imagine. They call them 'cheese' and 'yoghurt'. Strange! Five, they use my old fur, which I'm glad to be rid of, to make fur coverings for themselves. They haven't any of their own, you know. Six, they particularly like to ride me where my esteemed friend Horse (here she bowed gently) can't easily go. He's one for the swift charge, you know, the rapid assault, but his hoofs don't spread out like mine, and long marches in dry, sandy places are not at all to his liking. Am I correct, Horse?"

"Neighhhhhhh! Umph."

"I thought so. I can go for days and days and days without water. I can eat and even like all sorts of scrubby prickly things that other beasts don't enjoy. I can reach up and get the leaves and twigs off trees" (here she stretched her neck up very high and took a bite of the nearest branch, disturbing two sparrows and a nuthatch).

There was a pause while Camel chewed. She continued: "I was counting. What number was I up to please?"

"Eight!" chirped the Nuthatch, disgruntled.

"No, no, seven!" shouted several voices.

"Well, well, seven or eight, it doesn't really matter," said Camel. "The last point is that I am very nourishing and tasty, so I've been told. And then they make bags out of my skin to carry all their belongings in. I can't imagine why they have so *many* belongings, but I suppose it's because they're so naked all by themselves, poor things. Not very self-sufficient, you might say.

"In ancient times in the area they call Arabia, there was a place of rock and

sand, mountain and valley. In the valley there was water, but not a lot, and there was lovely grass for pasture. It was a good place for animals, and for people, too. In fact it was such a good place that the people there grew in numbers. They called themselves the Thamud.

"I came to them in a special way. I was not the property of anybody. I was truly myself, the property of God alone. I was big, and very beautiful, and free, and I came at the call of their prophet, Salih. He was a man from among them, but he was much nicer than most of the others.

"I used to watch them and listen to them when they came near the pasture assigned to me. They were of two sorts. One kind rode, they seldom walked. They had on all kinds of skins and fur and feathers. They used to look at me with angry faces, their mouths turned down at the corners. They kept their hands closed up, in fists.

"The other kind had very simple skins on, maybe not even skins but coverings made of plants of some sort. They were thinner than the first ones. They seemed hungry. I used to give them my milk whenever I could. They were very, very happy to get it. The other humans were not happy when I did this, however.

"When I first came Salih talked to them all about me. He made it very clear that I was God's camel, and didn't belong to anybody. He said God had sent me as a sign for them. They had to leave me alone! There wasn't a lot of water, as I told you, so they were to let me have it one day and take it for themselves the next. I understood that if they could leave me alone, and share the pasture and water with me, Salih would know that they had become more generous. He would also know that they had agreed to obey God's order. But if they didn't, or couldn't, there would be big trouble.

"Some of the people there understood what Salih was saying. They used to come to look at me, and even touch me, and talk about my being from God. I liked them; as humans go, they were polite. And I felt in no danger from them. They came and went and we didn't bother one another.

"But some, I didn't feel easy about. I used to watch them, when I wasn't eating

that good grass. They were quite clever. They had found a way to make shelters for themselves in the mountains. They had other people do the work, of course, while they watched. The people hit the rocks of the mountain with heavy things and sharp things and made holes in them. They hit them until the holes were very large and people could go inside. Around the edges of these holes they did a lot of work. I don't know what it was for, but it looked very interesting. They cut tree-shapes and flower-shapes into the stone. On the inside they went on banging and cutting and hauling out rocks for a long time, and I suppose the holes were getting very large and complicated. But I couldn't see. Then they would bring a lot of things inside and they would go in and live there.

"One night, when it was dark and most of the people were sleeping, I heard low human voices by the edge of the pasture. I listened. "

"I don't believe what Salih is saying about this camel."

"I don't believe what he says about *anything*!"

"I think he has made it all up! He just doesn't like to see us richer than he is. He tells us to be more generous! What for?"

"I think he wants to change our good old religion so he and his god and their gang can get power and tell us what to do!"

"Nobody is going to tell *me* what to do!"

"How could a god send a camel? Gods don't send camels!"

"And it drinks too much water, there's not enough for us!"

"And I saw some of the peasants drinking its milk!"

"What? I *sell* them milk!"

"Do you think it's dark enough now?"

"Yes, let's do it!"

"Before I knew what was happening, they were upon me. Someone swung a sword, and I felt my legs give under me and I was down. They made short work of me after that. Then one of them shouted out, 'Hey, Salih! We've killed your god's camel! Now you punish us if you can!' I lay dead in the field, and they went away, laughing about how they had managed to get away with it.

"I could still hear, and I soon heard people around me. Some of them were

angry, some were crying. I heard Salih's voice. He sounded as if he were angry and crying both at once. He said, 'You will only enjoy life in your homes for three more days. You can do nothing about it!' Then I heard him gathering around himself his friends and followers, and they left. I don't know what happened after that."

There was an interruption from high in one of the biggest trees, and Hawk flew down to Lion's rock. "Excuse me," he said courteously. "I believe that I know the end of your story."

"Sir," said Camel equally politely, "I should be indebted to you if you could tell it. I have always wondered what happened, and how God punished those people!"

"He sent them a mighty punishment," said Hawk slowly. "I was flying high over the territory of Thamud. The air was very still and I was having difficulty finding any currents. The sky was a strange shade of yellow and I felt uneasy. Something was about to happen. I was seeking a landing spot, peering down, and I was just over that city. I remember seeing you lying there, Camel, and wondering why. And then, beneath my eyes, the earth gave a shake! The ground went out of focus for a moment and seemed to open and come together again. In the moment before I was caught in a tremendous updraft, and literally blown away, I saw the rock caves and houses of those humans falling to earth, sending great clouds and billows of dust into the air. I'm sorry, after that I was too busy navigating to observe any more." Hawk bowed and retired from the rock.

"I am most grateful," said Camel formally. "I have always admired you, Hawk, and your keen powers of observation. You are probably the only survivor of the destruction of Thamud, except for Salih and his companions, who I heard going away. I hope they found a better home far from that place!" Camel sat down in the sand, smiling.

Sheep and  All Her Family Make Trouble

Sheep did not know it, but she met three prophets. The Prophet Solomon was David's son. Sheep's first story tells us about something that involved the two of them, when Solomon was still a boy but already wiser even than his father. Her second story describes the arrival of Moses among the people of the desert. He was fleeing Egypt because he had killed a man by accident. He had no home and no place to go to, so he must have been glad when some girls took him to their father, Jethro, who became Moses' teacher.

Recording Angel

"Goat, please come here!" mooed Cow. "I'm having all sorts of difficulty with Sheep. I'm trying to persuade her to get up and tell one of her stories – she has at least three – and she won't do it. She's so shy that even here in the Place of Perfect Peace, she's incapable of public speaking. Whatever shall we do?"

"Oh please Cow," bleated Sheep, "I don't want to. I can't. I'm too nervous. All those, those...you know, lions and things. It's too much. Leave me alone, dear Cow. Nobody wants to hear my stories anyway! Baaa-a-a-a!"

"Oh, come on, Sheep," laughed Goat. "There's nothing to be afraid of! Those blokes won't hurt you! You can relax! This is Paradise, girl! Lie around! Eat grass! Love your neighbours! They don't *need* to hunt us any more. Look, I know, how about if Cow here, and I, your old friends, come up with you and sit on either side. Would that make you feel better? Huh?"

Sheep considered the matter. She was naturally timid, but she was also naturally sociable. She definitely believed there was safety in numbers, and she didn't want to disappoint her friends. So, putting on her bravest face and trying to smile, she agreed to go, on two conditions.

"You have to promise to stay with me," she said. "One on either side. And I don't want to stand anywhere near Lion or Wolf. Dog, yes, I've been friends with Dog. In fact I'd feel safer near him than anywhere else."

"Got it," said Goat. "Let's go. Cow, you take the right side between Sheep and the big fellows. I'll take the left. And we'll go over there, near Dog, so he can protect Sheep and make her feel safe. Ready, now?"

They escorted a quivering sheep over to Dog's flower bed. Dog woke up. "Oh ho!" he said. "The call to duty! A sheep to protect! Ta-ra ta-ra!" He trotted around the little group, wagging his tail and sniffing the earth. "Coast's clear. No predators in striking distance. No poachers, rascals, scallywags or rustlers anywhere about. At ease, troops. I'll take guard duty." And he sat down, pleased and panting.

Cow nudged Sheep. "Go ahead, dear. It's time. I'm right here."

"I...I've never spoken *alone*," Sheep said in a soft voice with a nervous edge to it. "I've always been with my family. I...I don't know which story to tell. If you don't mind, I'll sort of put them together."

There were soft murmurs of encouragement from the group.

"You've been telling such interesting stories about yourselves and the prophets that – that I thought I would tell you about them too. I have three little stories. This is the first one:

"One night a group of us found a gate open. One of the more adventurous went through it, and a few followed, and then all the rest of us naturally came along. We discovered a lovely field on the other side. It was full of flowers and grass and plants. We rejoiced and began to eat, and the lambs began to play. We wandered around all night in that garden, and I suppose that what we didn't eat, we stepped on.

"The next morning, the owner of that field came to visit it, and found us there. Most of us were asleep. He was very upset. I remember waking to the sound of his angry voice ordering us out. We scrambled to our feet and ran off the way we had come, baaa-ing and calling, back to our home fields.

"The owner of the field came and talked with the man who looked after us. He was still angry, and at last the two of them went off together 'to see about it.' They took us along too, for 'evidence', whatever that is. They took us out of the fields, into town and right up to a big building they called the king's palace. We didn't know what was happening. We just stuck together.

"At the palace we saw the king. His name was King David. He had his boy with him, too. His name was Prince Solomon, and he was a nice looking young man. In fact, I almost felt he understood us as we were talking to one another, but I wasn't sure. I know he did, now, after hearing Hoopoe's story.

"The man of the field and our man got up and talked to the king. First one talked, then the other, then the first one talked again. The king listened carefully. Then he said something that made the angry man happy, but it made our man put his hands over his face and make funny noises.

"Then the young one spoke to the king, his father. I liked him, so I was listening and I heard him say some things like 'not fair' and 'too harsh' and 'he'll be ruined' and 'how about a trade?' When he had finished, his father looked at him the way a ram looks at his flock in the springtime – with great pleasure. Then the king spoke.

'The owner of the field shall have the sheep for a year. He shall have whatever the sheep make and what he gets from them: milk, wool, lambs. The owner of the sheep shall have the field for a year, to care for it and plant it, and make it green and growing again. After a year, they shall trade back and things will be as they were before.'

"The two men seemed quite surprised and happy. I think they felt it was fair. They thanked the king and his son. The field man then took us away, and our old man went off to take care of the field. We went on as usual without much difference at all.

"That's the end of one story. Do you really want another, or shall I sit down?"

"More, more!" called the animals, who were very pleased by Sheep's modesty and wanted to encourage her. So, with a bit more enthusiasm, she went on.

"Another time we were grazing in the sparse grasses of the Sinai Desert near

a place the people called Madyan. We were being shepherded by two girl people. They would take us out in the day to find something to eat, and bring us back at night to their father's tent. In the springtime they would cut our thick winter wool away and make things with it. They drank our milk and sometimes ate our meat. In return they looked after us and kept us safe from...from (and here Sheep looked warily over at Wolf and Lion, and then looked down and continued without mentioning their names).

"We used to get very thirsty. There were deep holes nearby that the people could get water out of. The girls used to take us to that place, but we always found a lot of other sheep there, and camels, and goats, and people. While it was nice to see our friends and relations, we really wanted to drink. Every time the girls tried to push their way in to the watering place, the other flocks and the men would shove them away. They were frightened, and stood aside, waiting. They waited and waited, and we got thirstier and thirstier. This happened many times. We were always the last to drink.

"Then one day there came a strange man out of the desert. We had never seen him before. He came up to our girls while they were holding us back away from the wells, and he said, 'What's the matter with you?'

"Our girls looked at the ground. They were shy, like me, I suppose. They answered him, though. 'We can't water our animals until the herdsmen drive theirs home, because we are weak and our father is a very old man.'

"Then that strange man called to us and led us and got through all the other men. He was big, and strong, and young. He was a real ram of a man and he got us right to the water and we drank our fill. It was wonderful. We loved him almost as much as we loved the water. Then he took us back to our girls, who thanked him, and he went away and sat down somewhere in the shade of a tree. Our girls took us back to their father's tent and I heard them telling their father all about it. Their voices sounded excited and happy. Then their father told them to go back and invite that man to dinner. One of them did. And he came.

"Everything was different after that. He stayed with us, and he married one of the girls, and he took care of everything. I learned his name was Moses. He was the strongest man I have ever seen. One time he went away. I think the story of Snake explains that. I saw him again later, but he wasn't herding us any more. He had a big herd of people instead. I think he must have missed us sometimes. We loved him more than they did.

"Now, my friends who have so kindly listened, I thank you."

"Wait, wait!" said Goat. "You have another story, the most important one! You have to tell about the Ram!"

"Oh Goat, I can't tell Ram's story for him! You must ask him to tell it himself. He went off alone in the mountains but, if you and Dog go and find him, I think he would come back. Dog, you will help, won't you? You have such a wonderful nose and you're so strong! I just can't talk any more."

Ram's Sacrifice

You know that Ishmael was the first-born son of Abraham. Ram's story describes Abraham going with Ishmael to sacrifice him, because God ordered him to do it. This happened on the plain and mount of Arafat, in Arabia. The devil appeared three times to them while they were going to the place of sacrifice.

Recording Angel

The mighty Ram stood before them. Unlike timid Sheep, he was bold, strong and proud. His great golden horns swung around his head and caused the muscles of his neck and shoulders to bulge with their weight. He gazed at the company with his brilliant amber eyes. His voice, when he spoke, was full of compassion and knowledge.

"I am a sacrifice," he said calmly. "I have died many, many times for the sake of God. Every pilgrimage, I am given again. I will tell you how this came to be.

"Like Camel, I entered my story as a gift from God. I had no other master. I was a wanderer in the high hills and the far deserts until, one day, I was told to go to a rocky mount in the middle of a great plain. I crossed the plain in the early morning. There was little to eat on it, and less to see. I reached the mount and bounded from rock to rock until I was standing on its top. There was an open space there, and on it was a large flat rock. I thought I was meant to stand on the rock, but I was told to leap down, and to hide myself further down the mount, in a small group of scraggly bushes. There I went and there I waited for further instructions.

"The sun came up and it grew very hot. To amuse myself while I waited, I looked all around over the plain. But in that whole morning I spied only two gazelles, moving rapidly away to the south, and one falcon riding the thermal

82

winds far overhead. It was a desolate spot. It was like the end of the earth. I wondered why I was there.

"After what seemed like a very long time, I saw some movement on the horizon. It was quite faint and I couldn't tell if it was man or beast. I kept watching, and after a while I made out two tiny figures. They seemed to be coming in my direction. I thought, 'Perhaps they are my reason for being here!'

"Then I saw another figure off to their left. By this time I could be sure the first two were humans. The third one I wasn't too sure about. It resembled a human, but its edges were unclear. They seemed to be shifting and adjusting, almost as if the thing were trying to pull itself together. And, while the first two were tramping along in a normal human fashion, this one kind of floated. It also seemed to be changing size all the time. I blinked my eyes and stared harder, but I couldn't focus on it. So I went back to watching the first two. They seemed very bright. In fact, as they came closer, they got brighter and lighter. I felt my heart beating faster as I watched them.

"I looked back at the other one. It was clearly heading towards the two humans, intending to intercept their way. Indeed, in a few moments, the three were together. They stopped, and the strange one was gesturing and, I suppose, speaking. Then the bigger of the light ones reached down to pick something up off the earth, and seemed to throw it at the other. They were very far away so I couldn't be sure of what exactly was going on. Oddly, without going anywhere, the stranger disappeared.

"Funny I should call him, or it, a stranger. But I already felt my heart calling to the bright ones, and the other didn't please me. It felt like a contradiction, something that disturbed the calm emptiness of earth and sky. The bright ones didn't disturb. I continued to watch them. They were closer now, and I could make out that one of them was taller and older and the other shorter and younger: a man and a boy. I could tell all this from the way they walked. We rams are very aware of the movements of feet and hoofs and paws.

"Then off to their right, this time, I saw that figure again. It felt the same, but it looked different. It was much bigger, and more focused. It was trying to look

like them, but instead of a brightness, all it could achieve was a kind of muddy glow. It moved across their path and once again tried to stop them, but they didn't stop. That is, they stopped only long enough to reach down to the earth and pick up some stones and throw them at the thing, whatever it was. Once again, it just disappeared. I felt the hairs on the back of my neck rising, and I snorted and pawed the ground. Still I watched.

"The bright ones were coming nearer. I could see them quite clearly now. I saw that the man had his hand on the shoulder of the boy. He had a lot of hair on his face, and it was white like mine. He seemed quite old, but his step was strong and sure. The young one had to go fast to keep up with him, but he managed. They came along toward the mount and had almost reached it when, Wham! there was an explosion and there was that creature again, bright red this time and breathing smoke and fire! I could hear its voice, very smooth and oily, talking about the earth, and riches, and gold, and other things I didn't understand. Both humans stopped, picked up stones, and threw them at him, hard. In a puff of black and purple smoke, he disappeared. For a few moments there was a terrible smell, like the smell of old eggs which have been cracked and abandoned in the nest.

"Then it was gone, and the sky and earth were clear again, and the silence returned. It was broken only by the sound of trudging feet and laboured breath, as the two came up the mount. They were on the opposite side from me by the time they reached the top, so they didn't know I was there. Although I wanted to be with them, I knew inside that I had to stay where I was and wait. How do we know these things?

"They took off their cloaks and I saw that the man had a long knife with him. We rams know these knives, for they use them when they sacrifice us. The two of them stood talking together, and then they raised their hands and talked to God, because I heard His name over and over. Then they came close and wrapped their arms around each other. Then the old person laid the young one down on his face, and uncovered his neck. The boy followed the man's directions without any hesitation, as if he knew exactly what was happening.

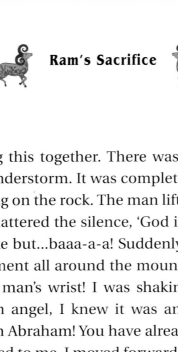

Clearly, they were doing this together. There was a charge in the air like the feeling just before a thunderstorm. It was completely still. I scarcely breathed.

"The boy was still, lying on the rock. The man lifted the great knife, called out in a loud voice which shattered the silence, 'God is Great!' and his arm started downwards on the stroke but...baaa-a-a! Suddenly there was a flash of light, a surge of power, a movement all around the mount and look, there was a great light-being holding the man's wrist! I was shaking all over. So were the two humans! It was truly an angel, I knew it was an angel, and it spoke in the language of humans: 'Oh Abraham! You have already done what God wanted!'

"The angel then pointed to me. I moved forwards, for this was my moment of glory. I was to replace the boy. I, not the human, was to be sacrificed and give my life to God. I was frightened, but I didn't care. I'd follow God's wishes. And then I had a deep, deep understanding. There at the rock, gazing at the marvellous angel and the two bright humans, I understood that those people had a choice. They had to decide to be there. I had been ordered, and I came. No question about it. God was sure of me, but the people had to come of their own free will, to show they were sure of God. And I put my neck out and the angel took the knife...once again I heard the cry, 'God is Great!'...and I was gone.

"It was a wonderful death. Now, look, here I am again, whole and strong, telling the tale. It's all very mysterious. Because of Abraham, every year I and others are sacrificed. We don't mind, we return again, and many people eat our blessed food.

"So thank you, my lovely ewe, for introducing my story. I think you had better come away with me now, and let me introduce you to the ways of Paradise, until you become stronger and less timid. Come on, dear!"

Sheep had been weeping at the end of Ram's story, and everyone knew she had felt it deeply. But she hadn't run away or hidden. She hadn't even leaned on Goat or Dog or Cow. Now she gazed at her friends with her large, wet, golden eyes, sniffled a little, glanced quickly at Ram, looked at the ground, made up her mind, and suddenly walked gracefully out into the field. He came to meet her, nuzzled her a little, and led the way through the circle of animals, which opened

up to let them pass. A few moments later Dog, who had watched the longest, saw them leaping about in the grass and flowers like a couple of spring lambs.

"So," said Dog, satisfied. "Leave them alone and they'll come home...I never really believed that before. Usually you have to go out in the rain and wet and find them. Must be the air; Sheep seems positively transformed! Good thing, too. No need to be timid here. Who's next?"

"I think I am," said Cow slowly. "I've been trying all this time to decide. Yes, I'll tell my story tomorrow."

Beautiful Cow

Cow's story is very, very famous. It is about how people make things hard for themselves by asking too many questions and by putting off doing what should be done. There are other stories about Cow, too, but she chose this one.

Recording Angel

It was early morning. Dew lay on the heavenly grass, and the flowers were just beginning to open their faces to the light. Cow took a mouthful of green blades, chewed them thoughtfully, and took another. She was remembering mornings somewhat like this on earth, when she and her friends would graze their way slowly across the hills, stopping often to chew their cud and look around. Sometimes they would stop all together to rest under the shade of some great tree.

"It's like that here," she mused, "only different. The grass is, well, greener. And the flowers more tasty. And I'm sure my milk has more cream!" She chewed a little more. "I could tell them about the golden calf. But that is a disgraceful story, and it's not about me. That calf wasn't real." She munched. "I could tell them about the dream interpreted by that blessed man Joseph, because there were many cows in it. But those were dream cows and not real, either. No, I think I'll stick to what I decided yesterday. I'll tell them about the cow described exactly by God." That settled, she went on with her breakfast, at peace with herself and the world.

The other animals arrived in ones and twos, greeted one another, and sat down. When Lion came, Cow stopped munching. She blinked her great eyes at the assembly, mooed quietly, and shook her head gently from side to side. Some

of the animals noticed for the first time how beautiful she was. They saw the softness of the inside of her ears, and the shine on her horns, and the muscles rippling under the smooth skin of her legs and haunches. They saw the sweetness of her colouring and the calm depth of her eyes.

"Yes, my dear friends, I am beautiful," said Cow softly. "Beautiful, and very useful and helpful to everyone. When people used to take me out to pasture in the early morning, seeing the new light and hearing the birds sing in time to the soft squish of my footsteps, they were very happy. I do like to be happy and peaceful myself.

"It makes my milk sweeter and definitely suits my disposition to have things very uneventful. I didn't mind sharing my life with people, so long as they were regular in their habits. You know, up at dawn, fed, milked, off to the field at a leisurely pace, home, milked, clean straw, that kind of thing. I became agitated and upset when the people or beasts around me did anything to disturb the regular, calm, even rhythm of the days and nights in which we lived.

"Well, I am going to tell you a story today. This story is about some people who couldn't accept this simple flow of everyday life. They insisted, every chance they got, in making life difficult and complicated. I used to watch them arguing. I could eat my whole breakfast and chew my cud while they kept on discussing some little thing. I didn't care to listen much but, sometimes when they were close and I had nothing better to do, I would pay attention to their arguments.

"These people had a leader, the prophet Moses. He had a really hard job. I felt sorry for him. I could see him trying to get his herd to do this or that, and they used to argue about everything! I don't know why he was so patient. A bull of my people would just come over and butt any cattle who behaved like his. But he kept on trying and trying. He used to lose his temper now and again, and then everybody would get scared and run around in circles like calves in a storm. Then he would calm down and things would go on as before.

"We used to travel about in a big area which had a lot of sand and bare earth and not very much good pasture. However, we animals did all right because

God kept sending us food one way or another. The people used to go out every morning and gather up theirs from the ground. They had little birds to eat, as well. Weren't they something like you, dear?" Here Cow looked over at a nearby bush, where a family of quail were nesting. One of them looked out and nodded, then went back to tending her children.

"You would think, wouldn't you, that people would be happy if they had all their food given to them, like cows, and didn't have to run around looking for it? These people weren't happy. Some of them told Moses that they wanted cucumbers and onions (ugh! they make my milk sour) and things like that. They didn't have the stomachs for heavenly food. Complain, complain, complain.

"Well, anyway, one day I was browsing in a field near the camp – they all lived in tents, you know – and I saw Moses coming towards a group of men. He was walking in that way he had when there was something important to say. He'd take big steps and stride along leaning on his staff with his beard streaming out behind. When people didn't want to hear some new law or news they would hide from him. These men pretended to be very busy, but he interrupted them anyway.

"Moses came right to the point. 'God commands you to sacrifice a cow,' he said.

"The men said, 'Are you making fun of us?'

'God save me from being an ignorant fool!' replied Moses.

"The men considered for a minute. I chewed my cud and listened. Finally they came up with a plan. So they said to Moses, (may God grant him patience), 'Pray to your Lord to make it clear to us *which* cow!'

"Moses went away and I suppose he prayed and then he came back and said, 'Look here, He says it is to be a cow neither too old nor too young, but of an age in between. Do, then, what you have been told to do!'

"I thought about my age and decided I was neither old nor young.

"The men mumbled together about this new information, and then they said, 'Pray to your Lord to make clear to us what *colour* she is!'

"Moses went away and I suppose he prayed again and then he came back and said,

'Listen, He says: "She should be a fawn coloured cow, bright and rich in colour, pleasing to those who look at her."

"I looked over my shoulder and down my sides and sure enough, I was exactly that.

"The men whispered again and then they said to Moses, (may God grant him huge amounts of patience),

'Pray to your Lord to make it clear to us *what she is to be like*, for to us all cows look like one another.

"Moses went away and I suppose he prayed again and then he came back and said,

'Indeed, He says it should be a cow not broken-in to plough the earth or to water the crops, without anything wrong with her, and without markings of any other colour!'

"I looked up and down my legs, switched my tail, glanced over my back and under my belly, and pranced around in a few circles to see if there were any other colours on me, but I couldn't see any. I must say I never had ploughed a field or pulled any water. That's tiresome work, going up and down pulling a thing that cuts into the ground, or going around and around and around some well, making a rut in the earth from stepping in the same place so many times! No, thank you. Not I.

"At last those stubborn people had to admit that they knew what God meant. So they said,

'At last you have brought out the truth!'

"But they weren't happy. I was valuable to them, you see. They liked my milk and my beauty, they liked the calves I made and they had ideas about putting me to work soon. They didn't want to give me up. But what could they do? So they led me away, and they sacrificed me as God had commanded. I didn't mind any more than Ram did, but I wish Moses had done it himself, as I liked him a lot better than the others. Anyway, that's my story and here I am!"

"My dear cousin," said Ox, "come and graze with me. We have shared so many of the same experiences on earth, let's talk them over between bites out in that

marvellous green pasture."

"How lovely," mooed cow. "I believe I see buttercups, and daisies, and cowslips! No onions, thank heaven, and no stubborn people to listen to. This is Paradise!" And off they went together.

Lion, meanwhile, was having some trouble with a buzzing in his ear. He kept shaking his head, which made his great mane fall in golden ripples, and he tried to scratch his ear with his paw. He scratched so hard that he rolled off his rock, shouting, "Do come out of there! I can't hear what you're saying because you tickle too much!"

A black and golden bee flew out of Lion's ear and perched on a nearby rose-bush. "I'mmm on tommmorrow," she buzzed.

Bee's Story and Spider's Web

"Can't you sit still?" said Lion, trying to keep his eyes on Bee, who was buzzing here and there in constant movement. "I'mmm busy!" hummed Bee, sucking on a violet, "I'mmm buzzzzzy! Lots of honnnnney nnnnneeded herrrrre! Rrrrrivvvvvers of honnnnney! Gobs and goblets of honnnnney! Who do you think is mmmmmaking it, mmmmmh?"

"I can't stand it!" roared Lion. "Look here, Bee, if you really want to tell us your story, you've got to quiet down a little. And stop buzzing so much! We're just not up to your speed. Some of us just woke up and – (looking at dog)- some of us are still asleep! This is Paradise! Can't you relax?"

"Nnnoo," said Bee, making an enormous effort to stop buzzing. "It isnnn't like that at all. You don't channnge in Paradise! You get mmmorrreso!" She flew around in rapid spirals. "You get to beee mmmorrre who you arrre! Once a busy beee, always a buzzzy beee, and I love it!" She did six somersaults and landed on Lion's nose. "But I'll trrry," she said.

"From the very beginning, God made His orders clear to the firrrst beee and all otherrr beees,

'Prepare for yourselves dwellings in the hills and in the trees and in the things people make for you. Then eat of all the fruits, and follow humbly the ways ordered for you by your Sustainer.'

"What could beee simplerrr thannn that? Make a place to livvve: you havvve three choices. Eat: you can eat all the frrruit, and the flowerrrs, too. Follow God's orrrderrrs, and He will take carrre of you. No morrre, nnno less. I'm *trrying* not to buzzz, Lion, but it's harrrd!

"So we set about doing it, and I shall describe to you what we did. Some of us

94

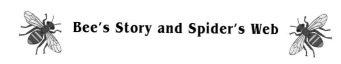

went to the high hills. We buzzed around there and found wonderful cracks and crumbled ledges on the sides of old cliffs. We made our wax houses there for our queens, and filled them with honey. We made spacious rooms for the new bees and for storing the honey, and we knew just how to do it. God taught us. He put it in us. We knew the shape, and it was the perfect shape, and it's still the perfect shape. It has six sides, all equal. Each little room connects perfectly to the next little room. You can go on building them forever, they always connnect! Nnnothing betterrr! So sommme of us livvved there.

"Sommme others of us went to live in trees. Ahh, the honey trees! We sought out old ones, dead ones, trees rotten in the middle. The best ones were those that had been hit by lightning and were still standing. They have a smoky smell that makes the honey delicious. We built in the holes and hollows of the trees, and filled them with honey and pollen and bees.

"Some more of us found straw things that people made for us. We made a deal with the people. They kept the houses strong and safe. We gave them some of our honey. (We are so busy we always make extrrra.) Later the humans experimented with wooden boxes and other houses. I didn't like any of those very much; I'm a tree girl myself. But some liked themmm. Lion, you really mmmust let mmme buzzz! I'mmm feeling all choked up!

Bee looked so sick that Lion felt sorry for her. "OK," he purred, "But keep it down to a low roar, if you please. It makes my ears twitch and my tail thump. And do try to sit still!"

"About the honnney," buzzed Bee. "I wannnt to tell you about the honnney!" She was quivering with excitement. "I eat flowerrrs, rrright? And frrruit. They go innnto mmmy belly and what commmes out? Honnney! It all depennnds onnn what I eat. If I eat wild flowerrrs – yes, Lion, I'm trying! – if I eat wild flowers the honnney is dark, the colour of amber sap from an old pine tree. If I eat clover blossoms, it is light, the colour of golden ripples on the water at dawn. If I eat the flowers of the orange tree, the honey is yellow like the sun. The colours and tastes of the honey are one of the pleasures of Paradise, and I hope you are all enjoying yourrrselvvves herrre!

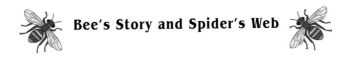

"Nnnow if you will excuse mmme, evvveryonnne, I'mmm busssy!"

Bee flew around Lion's head buzzing very loudly, and Lion put his paws over his ears and shook his mane violently. Then Bee was gone.

While everyone was looking around and wondering what happened to Bee, a new, small voice was heard from overhead. It sounded very thin and drawn out, coming through the air like the highest note of a tiny violin, the sound of a sunbeam in an old forest.

"If you have just a few moments," whispered Spider, "I'd like to show you my web..."

It was fantastic. What had been started before the very first story now stretched for yards and yards overhead, catching the light and reflecting it from thousands of silver threads. Its highest point sprang from the branch of a huge and lofty oak. Spider must have swung from the oak to a nearby beech, connecting to a high branch and then falling to a low one. Then she had swung back to a lower branch of the oak, and then climbed back to the upper branch again, making a huge square. The web, as it grew between these anchoring threads, hung, quivering, at a slight angle to the ground. Secondary threads travelled between the main ones, forming a nearly perfect octagon.

On this great eight-pointed star, Spider had begun her art. She had spun an outer border of tiny squares. Inside this was a row of triangles, some empty, some full. Inside these were seven plain bands of thread. Inside that Spider had begun her greatest effort. Since she could only go in straight lines, but wanted to create the illusion of a curve, she had made a series of tiny hops from thread to thread, each time changing her direction slightly. The result was loop after loop of web, and somehow she had been able to add colour to her spinning so that the loops changed from one hue to another of the rainbow, until they came full circle, and the red went into the violet and began again.

In the very centre were three bands of silver, and a shimmering dot of gold. On this dot sat Spider herself. "It is the frailest of houses," she said. "It will probably break very soon. That doesn't matter, for my delight is in the building. The process of perfection is what matters to me. As it serves its purpose in my

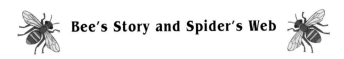

hunting, the web must be broken. But, when my effort is complete, just for this precious moment, I like to hang here and enjoy my handiwork. And in the spirit of our gathering, I wanted to share it."

The animals were awestruck. Each one had his or her beauty or art. But this heavenly web brought home to them once again where they were, and the wonder of their situation. They gazed and gazed, caught up and spun around by this beauty. And then Elephant stood up.

The tip of his left ear brushed the lower anchoring line of the web. It pulled, and stretched...and broke. The entire web, its tension lost, floated free and began to catch upon itself. Spider hung a moment more in the centre, and then scurried up one of the legs to the outer octagon, and from there to the oak tree. Looking down at the devastation, she said calmly,

"I think, this time, I'll try an icosahedron."

Elephant's Really Great Tale

Elephant is recounting his part in what happened when Abraha, leader of the Yaman, tried to attack Mecca and failed. That was in the same year as the birth of the Prophet Muhammad, which is known as the Year of the Elephant. Elephant is a great story-teller, and we will leave it to him.

Recording Angel

Elephant had been quite embarrassed by the events of yesterday. Elephants appreciate beauty very much. They themselves move with rhythm and grace, and recognise these qualities in other beings. Elephant had been so pleased by the results of Spider's weaving dance that he had wanted to have a closer look. As sometimes happens, he had slightly misjudged his height. Spider hadn't minded, but...Elephant had gone off with his ears drooping, and had spent the afternoon in silent reflection half-buried in the mud.

Finally, he had decided he could only make amends by telling a really great tale to wind up the meetings. There had been talk among the animals that it was time to stop, that they wanted to explore some other parts of Paradise, that maybe they could meet again next year, and so on. Elephant was slow to get going, and he had been waiting for just the right moment for his story. Now the time had come. He knew it was a good story, and he hoped he could do it justice. He rose carefully, and walked to the centre of the circle. Raising his trunk, he trumpeted.

Nothing brings the world to attention like the trumpet of an elephant. Lion lifted his head from his forepaws. Dog sat up and began to pant. Hoopoe flapped

her wings and squawked. Spider stopped at the juncture of the fifth and sixth legs of her new twelve-sided web, and dropped three feet to listen. Elephant began:

"I was a royal elephant," he stated grandly. "I was a royal elephant from the plains of Habash, and I was caught by men to serve their king. Since I was quite young, they were able to tie me and tame me to do their will. The trainers of elephants were wise in our ways, and they did not ask me to do things against my nature. They knew I was a kingly elephant, and they gave me kingly work to do. I was taught to lead, and I was taught to fight. I learned to set the pace for whole divisions of their army. My great feet were armed with sharp blades, and I learnt to slash and kick and squash the enemy. All that was not so bad. I felt like a partner, at least, in their ventures.

"However, they insisted I develop one unkingly characteristic. I was made to obey. If they wanted me to stop, I had to stop. To go, I had to go. I did not appreciate this training, and I squashed several of them – they are quite small, you know – under my feet. However, they pricked me in all the wrong places with their sharp thorn-things, and I hated it. So, to avoid the pricks, I did what they said. It was a small matter, after all. I felt, or so I explained it to myself, that I could always disobey any time I liked. I think the men knew this. They knew they had not broken my will. But I was a war elephant, not a tame elephant for hauling logs and carrying loads, and it was just as well to leave me a little wild. So they let me be. There was one man to care for my needs, and he slept in the straw beside me. He brought me good things to eat and talked softly in my ear. Except when I heard the wild elephants bellowing in the forest, I was content.

"After I grew older and reached my full size, which you see before you, messengers came, new humans wearing different skins. My man told me we were going to leave that place and cross the water. I love water. I imagined days of wading along the shores of lake after lake. I was wrong. We came to a place where the water lay ahead, and it was vast. It stretched as far as I could see and beyond. There was a kind of house floating on the water, and they wanted me to enter it. I had no intention of doing that. So my man spoke sweet words in my ear, and offered me good-smelling hay and fruits, if only I would walk up the

wooden path to this floating house. When his talk didn't work, they resorted to pricks again, and I was so hurt and insulted that I kicked one of them and walked up the path.

"It was a frightening experience. I am very heavy, and the wood creaked dangerously under my weight, and the house bobbed up and down. Then out of my deepest memories, I recalled my ancestors of the Ark, who had ridden so bravely for so long in just such a bobbing house. There were two of them, and I was one. I prayed this Ark was strong enough, and went aboard.

"We crossed the water and reached land when I thought there was no more land to reach. I descended on a similar wooden path and felt myself safe again on the good earth. My man was with me, and we entered a strange land. It had new smells, new light. Some of the humans made different sounds and had skin of a different colour. Otherwise, they were the same.

"I was put in a grand stall and given a lot of attention and many humans came to look at me. After some time I came to understand their speech. It seems I was to lead a great army and go north, over the mountains, to a place called Makkah. They spoke of it with awe. It was an old holy place. We elephants also have holy places. I listened carefully. This place had a thing in it called the Ka'abah. The king of these people where I was didn't like the Ka'abah. He wanted to smash it down. He wanted all the humans to forget that holy place and make a new place here, by him. He had built a huge building and was just waiting for the people to come. They didn't come, because they all went to the Ka'abah instead.

"Abraha was the king's name. He was a very determined person. He gathered his armies, and they made a great display of spears, banners, and armour. While they were lining up and getting ready, I was being decorated and armed. My tusks were sharpened and painted gold. White circles were painted around my eyes and tail. Sharp blades were attached to my ankles. Red, green and yellow stripes were applied to my body. I was led to the front of the army. The soldiers who had not seen me before were shaking and shrieking. I must have been a fearsome sight.

"I myself felt good, strong, and ready to lead. At last I had a true kingly role. I trumpeted my war trumpet, and we began the march.

"As we went along, we met one tribe after another. Some were armed and ready to fight. But when they saw me, they turned and ran in terror. You would think they had never seen an elephant before. I suppose they had not. My people are not native to their land. The sight of me, so much larger and stronger than they, must have made them feel insignificant. So we went on without a fight, over high mountains where the eagles soar and the water falls over cliffs. I was deeply satisfied to be free to move again, although they kept me at a slow pace.

"We came down from the mountains to an area of hills, beyond which we could see a great plain. There was little growing there; a place for camels, not elephants. I couldn't see why anyone would want to go there at all. We marched along.

"We reached the edge of a high bluff, the plain all spread out below. Far, far, in the distance I could see a human habitation, and in its centre was a square black shape. "That may be the Ka'abah," I thought to myself. "Perhaps I can destroy it by hitting it many times with my head." We camped in that place. Some people came up from below and went into the tent of the king. One of them seemed to be a king himself, I could tell by the way he walked and the way the soldiers backed away from him. I thought to myself, "Perhaps he has come to save his town and his holy place. He has no army, and no elephants. What can he do?"

"I heard the soldiers talking together. 'He says let the Lord of the Ka'abah save the Ka'abah!' laughed one. 'Where is this Lord, then? Can you see him?' They all laughed and went on sharpening their swords.

"It was time to descend. My man came to get me, and gave the order to rise. I stood up and took a step forward. I tried to take another – and could not move. I tried my back feet. It was as if they were rooted to the ground like trees. It was completely impossible for me to go forward. My man tried everything, including some of the painful pricking. It did no good, because movement was

beyond my power. Finally, he told me to turn around and go the other way. Easily, I obeyed, glad to find I could still lift my feet. He told me to turn around again and go towards Makkah. This I could not do. Others came to help him. They pushed, pulled, swore, hit me, poked me, shouted at me. They even pricked me with their swords. They were wasting their time. I understood.

"This really *was* a holy place. I was not supposed to go there. I was not stupid. Even if I could have, I would not have moved an inch towards the Ka'abah. I know Who gives the real orders! So I withstood their prods and my own pain, and did not waver.

"The king came out, and he was both angry and distressed. He paced up and down. He talked to me himself. He yelled at my man. He was at a loss as to what to do, and kings are not used to that. Then, it began to get dark, although it was only the middle of the day. A cloud of darkness rose from the west, and moved towards us. It was unnatural, strange, and I squealed in terror. My cries terrified the army, who were already very nervous. The cloud came nearer, and I could see that it was not a cloud at all, but a huge migration of birds, flying low. They held their legs down in a strange way, and seemed to be holding something in their claws.

"Then, they were upon us! The birds were right overhead, there was hardly any light, and sharp hard things began falling out of the sky! One or two touched me, but none broke my skin. I seemed to be protected from them. Perhaps the birds knew I was on their side, obeying Orders. But the men were hit, over and over again, and the stones hurt them. They ran in every direction to escape, but there was no escape. The horses and other beasts that were with us all ran away, and I decided to run too.

"As I turned and ran, away from Makkah, I saw the king. He had lost his turban, and was screaming to his guards, but they were taking care of themselves. I didn't see him again. I went, and the other animals went also, and we all escaped unharmed. Many of the men never left that bluff overlooking the plain. Many more caught up with us, and marched towards the south and home, but fell sick on the way. Most of them died, crumpled by the side of the

path. They had red spots all over them. I think their illness came from the hard things dropped by the birds. The king died, as well.

"I was unused to the wild life after all my years in captivity, and found little comfort in the vegetation and heat of that area. I got back at last to the city in the south, and found my way to my stall at the palace. I resumed my life there under the new king. Never again did we try to go north to Makkah. So that's how it was."

Elephant shuffled gently and gracefully away from the centre of the circle, and the animals moved aside to give him room. There was a lot of talk about his story, and a general stretching of backs and shaking of paws and wings, for it had been a long tale. Suddenly, there came a great whirring of wings, and a flock of birds flew low overhead, dropping something. Remembering the story, some animals cringed in fright, but soon recovered when they realised that what was being dropped were fruits of every colour imaginable. They were delicious, and their tastes went off like explosions in the animals' mouths and made them laugh and tumble over one another looking for more.

As they tumbled, and rolled, and somersaulted, and slithered, and hopped, and flew, and slipped, and ran down a broad green hillside, they came upon the surprise of Cow and Bee. Two shining rivers crossed the valley at the bottom, one ivory white and one of gold. Rivers of milk and honey, the foods of the Garden. The animals fell silent and bent their necks to drink. The goodness and wellness that filled their beings made them want to dance for joy. So in groups large and small, prancing or leaping, swooping or crawling, by whatever gesture came to them most naturally, they moved up the two river valleys towards the mountains beyond. Lion, far out in front, stopped and turned around. "Thank you for your stories!" he roared. "Until we meet again!" Horse galloped past. "Until we meet again!" he whinnied. "Peace be with you all!"

Here ends my record of the stories of the animals. It has been my pleasure to share it with you and to track their progress when they first met in the Garden. Should they meet again, in another time and space, I will be there to record, for that is my function. And I shall be sure to pass the stories on to you.

Recording Angel